Praise for

THE HAPPENSTANCES AT THE YELLOW COUNTY COMMUNITY SWIM AND RACQUET CLUB THE SUMMER BEFORE LAST

"Full of wit, charm, hilarious one-liners and clever digressions, Peter Harmon's Happenstances plays in a landscape of Americana reminiscent of John Hughes, but with tongue planted in cheek, pokes fun at familiar tropes and archetypical comedic characters while at the same time valuing all the elements enough to deliver a fresh and enjoyable summer read.

Poppy - and full of pop-culture references that'll have Millennials giggling out loud and sharing the text with their friends - Happenstances doesn't take itself too seriously while still respecting its readers, resulting in the perfect poolside read (and not only because it takes place at a pool!)"

- Jason Stefaniak, award winning filmmaker

"A sheer wave of nostalgia hits me in Peter Harmon's book. I am filled with both laughter and tears. Based on our childhood community pool, I am reminded of the pure joy of being a kid and figuring it out. Our pool was an idealistic dream for the American kid. The place where we had our first jobs, our first kiss and most likely our first sloppy joe. It was just happenstance that I happened to be there, and I would not change that experience for the world. Thank you Peter for taking me back to the good ole days! This is a book that I recommend to anyone looking for an endearing summer read."

- Gabrielle Christian, actress/ activist

"Forget what you think you know about the perfect summer break and allow yourself to high-dive into the heartbreak, exhilaration, and sheer madness that's waiting for you at the YCCSRC.

Peter Harmon's charming storytelling will make you believe for the first time in your life that the jerk, babe, nerd and outcast can actually come together to fight in the name of justice -- and, even more surprisingly, make you catch your breath when you realize they might possibly stand a chance."

- Jamie Petitto, writer and YouTube personality at Gurl.com

The Happenstances at the
Yellow County Community Swim and Racquet Club
the Summer Before Last
by Peter L. Harmon

© Copyright 2015 Peter L. Harmon

ISBN   978-1-63393-148-0

Published by

◤ köehlerbooks™

210 60th Street
Virginia Beach, VA 23451
212-574-7939
www.koehlerbooks.com

DEDICATION:

To my family, my friends who are as close as family, and the girl who ran away with me to start a new family.

The Happenstances at the Yellow county community Swim and Racquet club the Summer Before Last

PETER L. HARMON

VIRGINIA BEACH
CAPE CHARLES

PROLOGUE

THE SUN ROSE over the Yellow County Community Pool. Pinks and reds washed over the clear blue of the pool's over-chlorinated water. Clouds puffed out their chests, hoping to be noticed later by sky-gazers and compared to doggies or ducks or whatever general shape the wind had gently sculpted them into. Green shrubs lined the chain-link fence that surrounded the compound. A deck overlooked the pool area.

A sign on the fence read *Yellow County Community Swim and Racquet Club: Join Our Family Today!!1* The numeral *1* was a mistake. It was supposed to be three exclamation points, but the gentleman who had made up the sign wasn't the most computer savvy and had forgotten to hold down *Shift* when pressing the number one on the final exclamatory punctuation mark—rookie move.

Another sign proclaimed *Opening Day: May 27th, Memorial Day Weekend. Celebrate Our 50th Season!!* Not only had the person who made that sign quit while she was ahead and stopped at two exclamation points, but she also knew how to make the number's suffix tiny.

A snack bar sat in one corner of the compound, constructed of painted white cinderblocks. It was not necessarily a moneymaker for the club, but a necessity nonetheless as the closest place you could score a snack outside the pool grounds was over in the next town, strangely named Tuxedo, the kind of place where you wouldn't be caught dead wearing a tuxedo, unless of course, you were dead, and your hearse happened to drive down Tuxedo Road.

The snack bar provided not just frozen confections and over-syruped sodas, but the patrons really relied on the teens and tweens inside to prepare their meals for them, and that was never more evident than during the lunch rushes at promptly eleven forty-six in the morning and forty-six past noon when adult swim had just begun, and the hordes of sometimes shivering, skinny kids with chlorine-cowlicked hair would tug on their mothers' cover-ups, asking for a couple dollars to get mozzarella sticks or nachos or, God forbid, chicken quesadillas.

Beautiful brown clay tennis courts were a stone's throw away, where you would always find a few wheezers and geezers thwunking a ball back and forth, seemingly in slow motion. Twice a week the Yellow County Youth Tennis Team would don their white polos of varying sizes, much like the vastly varying skill levels of those who would participate, and compete against Brown Town Hall and Recreation or Bowie or Glenarden or even Crofton!

A guard office sat by the fence near the front entrance and locker rooms, where the lifeguards had a bird's-eye view over the pool so they could monitor safety issues, monkeyshines, or just scheme on that girl who came with her friend for the first time who none of them had made out with yet.

The crown jewel was a high dive jutting over the twelve-foot deep pool well, wearing a regal blue sash that connected the handrail to the support bars. There was a stretch of scratchy black tape on each step to grip the wet feetsies of those brave enough to climb them. When other swim teams visited for a meet, they looked up and coveted that thing, hoping, but not voicing it to their coaches, that there would be a free-swim time after the meet in which they could jump off of that freakin' awesome board.

Usually Memorial Day was a grand affair at the club. There would be a watermelon race where every member of a family had to be present to push a greased watermelon from one side of the pool to the other and back again. Invariably, the kids would beg their father to participate; Dad would balk, and Mom would have to put her flip-flopped foot down. Next thing you know, Daddy would be in the shallow end with his shirt on, rolling that watermelon, and he would get into it, recapturing a bit of the competitive edge he had back in high school. He would be picturing himself muscled up, wearing his sporting uniform instead of the now see-through off-white undershirt covering his beer belly.

Another favorite was the soda dive. Cans of soda were thrown into the deep end, some with dollar bills rubberbanded around them. Kids, separated into heats by age, would wait by the edge of the well, jockeying for position. Every once in a lifeguard's tenure, a child would slip or be pushed in before the starting whistle and the trigger-happy tots would all dive in before the *go* was given. But, if rules were followed and everything went as it was supposed to, the ultimate prize was the lukewarm root beer with a soggy dollar strapped to it—the dollar that the snack bar would receive only minutes later.

Yes, on Memorial Day there was a laundry line of drying singles hanging above the order window in the snack shack. They would dry a little crispy, be put into the register with the rest, and counted that night for the bank to receive.

Those crinkly dollars were the kings of the deposit bag. Sure, there are dollars that have been in more exciting places than the pool, singles especially, but those prize dollars could stand up straight, crack their backs, and tell their tales of deep water diving to the limp George Washingtons who were fresh from some tween's sweaty wallet.

CHAPTER 1

THAT PARTICULAR MEMORIAL Day morning started out not particularly memorably. A portly man in his thirties, with strong arms and back but a tummy devoid of definition, dove into the as yet unbroken, glasslike water of the pool, disrupting the calm. He swam a lap to and fro underwater without taking a breath, a dark-blue silhouette in the aquamarine. Either his legs didn't get the memo that his arms were doing the breaststroke, or his arms forgot to send it, because his legs were thrashing out behind him, making tiny bubbles in the water, in the style of free. He slapped the side of the deck upon completion. His head broke the water with a shake and a smile, and he climbed out of the water, droplets dripping off of his generous chest hair. He ran a hand through his chestnut-tinted hair and wiped his hand over his face, the already pruning tips of his fingers rubbing against his burgeoning laughlines. He opened his surprisingly blue eyes, the same color as the water, even though his features were dark.

The temperature would reach the mid-nineties that afternoon, but it was still early, and nipple-stiffeningly chilly.

The cool temp didn't hurry his hustle, as he casually stepped through the chill morning air.

His clothes were waiting for him on a nearby blue and white striped deck chair. He quickly toweled off, stepped into his red lifeguard-issue bathing suit, and donned a silver-colored whistle on a red lanyard. Over his head he pulled on his official Yellow County Community Swim and Racquet Club polo shirt. Size medium. A little snug. His name, Jonathan Poole, was stitched proudly across the left breast.

The stitching was done apathetically by an automated sewing machine over at the baseball cap shop. A minimum-wager had typed the letters of Jonathan's name into the template and selected the standard script font that was available for no extra charge (Edwardian Script, for example, was five cents more per letter, and when you're embroidering polos for the whole staff, that starts to add up), hit the 'any' key, and voila, created the personalized prize that Jonathan donned daily.

So no, the stitching itself and the stitcher were not too bowled over by their handiwork, but the stitchee, the one whose name beamed from this particular polo, was indeed proud of the shirt, and especially of the little letters underneath the name (two rows of stitching, that's a whole dollar extra per shirt) that read *Head Lifeguard In Charge*.

Jonathan moved through the small lifeguard office with purpose, deftly dodging the dangling whistles, saying a "How do you do?" to the CPR dummy (Tim), and putting a stack of binders under the cot that was pushed up against the wall facing the door.

Through that door entered "Wild" Bill Peterson, a man who discovered heavy metal late in life—thanks to the high-school-aged grandson he'd taken care of for a spell—and committed to it whole hog. He was in his mid-sixties but wore black band T-shirts, size large, for the large amount of *rocking* he did while wearing them. The shirt was decorated with electric chairs and axes, and its owner kept a head full of long, scraggly hair despite the yarmulke-sized bald spot on the top of his dome. Metal was usually blasting from Wild Bill's ever-present Walkman. He had that yellow one with the rubber grip. And at that moment he turned the volume wheel down a couple notches.

"Jonathan," Bill said.

Jonathan was startled. "Bill!" he said as if he had been caught polishing his whistle instead of in an office where he had every right to be.

"Got here a little early, didn't you? The newsletter said that the employee meeting wasn't until seven thirty today." Bill was more amused than confused. Of course, Jonathan was there early. This was his Christmas Day, and he would be more anxious than a tot trying to spy Santa Claus coming down the chimney.

"The newsletter?"

"The *Yellow County Community Chronicle*..."

Jonathan got on his game. "Duh, the *Chronicle*. I got that the other day...in my mailbox. I just thought I'd get an early start. I don't want anyone to be disappointed."

"I'm glad you're back. Isn't this your tenth summer?"

"Something like that." Jonathan knew the real answer; it was several more than ten.

"They all run together after you get to a certain age, don't they?"

Jonathan didn't respond, but they certainly did.

"What have you been doing the rest of the year?"

Jonathan hesitated. "You know, keeping busy."

"What is it you do in the off-season again?"

Jonathan opened his mouth to speak, not knowing really what his answer was going to be, but hoping he could trust his brain to think of something satisfactory before noises started coming from the hole in his face. But at that very opportune moment, the kind of moment that happens in a situational comedy or a film perhaps, when someone is going to speak when they don't want to, a thin young man whose parents hailed from India with a mop of black hair scurried by the guard office.

Roheed Mahaad was sixteen but looked quite a bit younger, and he didn't stop moving. He gave a little "Hello, sirs" as he passed along with the universal hand sign for *live long and prosper*.

"Looks like people are starting to show up," Jonathan offered, internally relieved.

"Rock on," Bill replied. There were things he didn't know, nor did he really care to know, about Jonathan. Bill's attitude about him was *heck with it*. Jonathan was a good lifeguard, and he didn't seem to want to divulge much about his personal life, which was *absitively posolutely* okay with the Wildman. He put his Walkman phones back on his head and cranked that sucker to twelve.

CHAPTER 2

CARS BEGAN TO fill up the Yellow County Community Swim and Racquet Club parking lot, the drivers mostly being dumb-looking teens with stupid haircuts, the tires of their parents' beaters that they let their sons and daughters borrow bouncing on the road, where tree roots had cracked and split the black asphalt. Middle-schoolers with train-tracked teeth walked from down the street where they made their moms drop them off.

Working at the YCCSRC was a rite of passage, a coming of age. One summer you were playing tennis baseball down by the volleyball court or soap hockey in the showers, then you blinked your eyes and boom, you were starting your first day of tennis court maintenance, then snack shack candy window, then grill window, then grillmaster, and then, Lawd willin', you were a licensed food handling snack bar manager, gazing out the window of the shack, craning your neck to catch an inning or two of the game, as board-short clad, shaggy-haired youths thwacked the neon balls with loaner rackets, trying to hit the ball over the big green wall with the stripe painted across it, the one where lonely gentlemen would hit balls to themselves, waiting for a doubles match that would never be.

On that first day, the chubby young bucks would pass through the locker room to enter the pool grounds, seeing the fresh soap sitting in the dish, and for just a moment think of taking that sucker down, grabbing a couple dudes, and having a full on soap hockey scrum, kicking the slippery bar across the wet tile. But then they would snap out of it, remember that they were now employees of the club, and trot away to begin their minimum wage entry into the working world.

Charlie Heralds pulled into the lot and parked in the far corner. He was a slim, handsome young guy wearing a full-length trench coat. He walked to the trunk of his car, looked around, and took off his dress socks.

His toes were webbed—not just a minor elongation of the flesh between a toe or two, but all-out Kevin Costner in *Waterworld*. He had asked his parents early on in life if they would get him the minor cosmetic surgery to de-web his toes and they had thought him too young, plus, his dad said, they would build character. Charlie always assumed that he would pay for the surgery himself when he had the cash and anyway he had Bing'd webbed toes and Wikipedia had said that Dan Aykroyd had webbed toes (I'm sure not to the extent of Charlie boy), and if it was good enough for Dan Aykroyd, it was good enough for young Charles. But that didn't mean he would ever walk barefoot down the drive to pick up the morning paper, no sir.

He unbuttoned the trench and exposed that it had a fake collar and tie sewn to the top and fake pant legs sewn to the bottom. There were even fake dress-shirt cuffs sewn into the coat's arms. He went from looking like a young man completely dressed for an office job to a late teen wearing board shorts and a YCCSRC snack bar manager shirt, size M on the tag, but it had been worn and washed enough times to fit more like a SMedium.

Charlie slipped old white socks and beat-up grey New Balances 420s onto his flippers and flopped them onto the cracked asphalt of the parking lot.

A flashy sports car passed, you know the kind, over five hundred horsepower with an automatic transmission. Charlie raised his brows at it. The vanity license plate read *1NNBR3D*.

The car parked and Florence Comfortinn stepped out. She was in her late teens and good-looking in an Instagram kind of way, smartly dressed in tennis casual. She walked into the compound through the guard gate.

Charlie was surprised that her camera crew wasn't with her as she was one of the cast members of a local web-based reality show, *Rich B Words of Yellow County*. But anyway, he didn't care too much so he threw the trench coat into his trunk, shut it, and made his way toward the guard gate, but a late '90s 'Stang blaring some repetitive dubstep beat sped too close to him, almost hitting him.

"Watch it, Judas!" he yelled.

The Mustang screeched into a parking spot and Judas Traditore stepped out, a large fraternity brother in a Beta Gamma Theta T-shirt, size large but tight in the sleeves to show off his large guns. He barely registered Charlie's complaint but gave an obligatory tug on his crotch and said simply, poetically, "Suck it."

• • •

A quick primer on the *Rich B Words of Yellow County*: The bi-monthly semi-scripted docu-drama web-series followed the social lives of five wealthy teens, most of whom went to East Yellow High. It was shot and edited by an EYHS junior, Jerd McKinley. Jerd originally started the show as a ruse to get close to the most popular girls he knew of, but soon he was swept up in the show's success.

He went from editing the series extracurricularly in his bedroom to being able to use the school's computer lab during a free period for an in-school internship credit. Jerd was savvy.

The show received some scrutiny, however, from the East Yellow High School newspaper, the *East Yellow Journal*, when one of the show's stars claimed she was a victim of "Frankenbiting," a term used in the reality television realm to describe chopping up a person's sound bites and reordering them to make the person appear to say a sentence that they never said, much like Dr. Frankenstein's monster was a creature created from a variety of human appendages that should have never been assembled.

Jerd deftly dodged the criticism, claiming it was typical *East Yellow* journalism. Nonetheless, the show was on hiatus for that particular summer.

• • •

As Charlie made his way through the guard gate, maybe two dozen teenaged staff members were already sitting at the picnic tables by the snack bar waiting for the meeting to start. Jonathan and Bill conversed. Florence texted furiously. Judas power-thrusted at some young female lifeguards. So everything was pretty much business as usual.

Charlie spotted Roheed sitting alone and made his way over to him. Roheed's eyes lit up when he saw Charlie, and they exchanged a conservative high-five, not really a low five, more of a mid-five, kind of a two and a half.

"Roheed, my man. What's been up over at North Yellow High?"

"I have just completed another year of high school."

"Hope you didn't get into too much trouble," Charlie joked.

Roheed didn't follow. "There was this one time in AP Calculus when the teacher thought I was programming formulas into my calculator because I kept getting perfect scores. But I wasn't, and it was all a big misunderstanding."

"I meant like getting arrested at a party or something, but whatever. How have the ladies been treating you?"

"Oh, they've calmed down with the name calling substantially."

That wasn't what Charlie meant either, but he let it go; Jonathan was making an announcement anyway.

"We're just waiting for a few more people," he said. "We'll start in a couple minutes."

Charlie, a little disappointed at the quality of Jonathan's announcement—I mean, why even stop everyone for something so trivial?—leaned back over to Roheed and asked, "Do you have a girlfriend? Have an occasional late night creep on the down-low?"

"Sadly, no. It seems intelligence and personality aren't necessarily what's trending currently."

Just then Judas stood up on a picnic bench to display his

extra-long whistle lanyard that he had modified to hang near his genital region.

He addressed his public, "Hey!"

Charlie nudged Roheed and said, "As if on cue..."

Judas continued, "Which one of you ladies wants to blow my 'whistle'?" He used his pointer and middle fingers to make big floating quotation marks in the air, as if he needed to.

Scattered laughter and groaning, in near equal measure, rippled over the young staff.

"Anyway," Charlie said, "maybe this will be your summer."

"Indubitably," Roheed replied.

Jonathan cleared his throat; the staff quieted. "Today is the opening day of the fiftieth season of the Yellow County Community Swim and Racquet Club. Bill here..."—Jonathan gestured to Bill, and Bill threw up a rock-on devil's horns hand signal—"is on the board that oversees this whole operation. He's my boss, and I'm your boss. My name is Jonathan."

One joker called out, "Hey, Jonathan," and some of his dumb middle-school buddies chortled.

Jonathan continued, "Now let me introduce your management staff. Judas Traditore is my lifeguard assistant manager." Judas smiled proudly, then began tweaking his nipples through his shirt when Jonathan looked away and continued with his spiel. "Charlie Heralds is the snack bar manager." Charlie waved humbly. "With his assistant manager Roheed Mahaad." Roheed gave the *live long and prosper* sign and said nothing.

"That brings us to our first new management employee in quite some time. She will be our new tennis court maintenance manager. May our former tennis court maintenance manager Harris rest in peace." He took a moment, breathed through his apparent sadness, and continued. "Let me introduce you to Florence."

Florence took a short break from texting to stand up and do a slight curtsy. Roheed's eyes widened, just noticing her for the first time. Charlie saw Roheed staring at Florence and took a small notebook—the kind you can get in a pack of five for a dollar—out of his back pocket.

And then Florence stood in a sundrenched field, tossing

her hair in slow motion as it shone softly, out of focus. The air smelled of fresh lilac and she was wearing medieval dress and wielding a foam LARPing sword.

Roheed appeared, dressed to the hilt in plastic armor. They began fighting, foam on foam, foam on plastic, until Florence brought her sword up in a mighty slice, hitting Roheed in the chest and bringing them both to the ground, Florence on top of Roheed. She poised to stab him with the rounded tip of her weapon.

They broke down into laughter. Florence smiled, "Talk nerdy to me."

She moved in for the kiss.

Charlie shook his head—Jonathan was droning on about safety in and around the pool, as he was apt to do.

"So like I said," Jonathan re-said, "there is no running on the pool deck, especially if the pool deck is wet, but the sticky wicket is that if the pool deck is too hot, it could also pose a problem—some toesies might get burnt. Or at least the hot deck will make children want to run from the deck to the pool, but they will inevitably slip and scrape their knees, so we have to take the bucket from off of the hook on the side of the pump shed and dump pool water on the deck to cool the deck down. And to add a degree of difficulty, the wet pool deck is slippery, so there is no running on the pool deck..."

Roheed of course was still staring at Florence, so Charlie bumped him with his elbow.

"Come on, man, Jonathan's talking about his hot deck again, but we open at eleven and all the dishes will be covered in dust from the off-season."

Roheed stopped staring, begrudgingly.

Charlie closed his notebook and tucked it back into his pocket, the line "Talk nerdy to me" written in block letters on one of the lined pages.

CHAPTER 3

AS JONATHAN CHECKED the pool's pH with a small kit, Judas, always putting his own flourish on the task at hand, sprayed off the pool deck with a hose threaded between his legs so it looked like he was urinating all over the place. If Judas had actually been making human lemonade, his acidic urine would have trickled into the pool and thrown off Jonathan's readings substantially because he had been pounding brews until the wee hours of that very morning. But fortunately for all involved, he was not peeing, just spraying some tepid water out of an old hose.

Speaking of an old hose, Bill kicked back and listened to his 'phones in the guard office.

On the clay tennis courts, Florence went along the boundary lines with a brush. She had already dragged the six-foot-wide court broom to and fro across the length of the six- court expanse. After the boundary lining she would turn on the sprinklers and give the clay a quick sip so they could dry before opening hour. If there was one thing she had learned at her parents' country club from the—her words—"kindly African-American gentleman who ran the facilities," it was how to maintain a clay tennis court.

What she never learned, or cared to ask for, was his name, but if you were to ask her, she would immediately say "Bagger Vance."

• • •

Charlie and Roheed stood by the massive three-basin sink in the snack bar and did the dishes.

Charlie washed. "I feel like I'm just on summer vacation right now, in a bad way."

Roheed dried. "What was graduation like?"

"Terrifying." Charlie shuddered.

"I saw some of the short films you made. They were funny."

"They didn't get into any festivals. They didn't get any hits on the Internet," Charlie said as if those goals were of equal weight.

"You just graduated high school. Maybe your aspirations are too high."

"Nobody knows who I am."

"Do you have anything in the works?"

"I'm working on a screenplay, or trying to. I don't have any good ideas."

Roheed dried a ladle with decades-old nacho cheese permanently caked on it. Charlie lowered his head. "I haven't finished my application to film school yet. I need a writing sample, and I've got nothing. I got a C in screenwriting...I'd rather not talk about it."

"My parents would kill me if I got a C."

Jill Bateman, a fourteen-year-old first-year snack bar employee, struggled with her hollow-boned bird arms to open an industrial-sized tub of ranch dressing. Her YCCSRC T-shirt was knotted on the side to expose a little bit of midriff, size XS for Xtra Sexiness. She hadn't quite figured out what to do with her hair yet and was all limbs and no torso, but that wasn't slowing her down.

Charlie watched Jill in his periphery to make sure she didn't make a mess. "Yeah, mine don't know yet. They think—" and sure enough, she got the ranch open and spilled it all over the floor.

Charlie grabbed some rags, handed one to Jill, and they began sopping up the creamy dressing.

Florence walked by the window. Roheed stared. Charlie got

up from the floor, returned to the dishes and continued washing. When he glanced back to check Jill's progress, she was bending over, rag in hand. She looked over her left shoulder at Charlie, enticingly. She put her finger in the spilled white liquid and licked it in a way that she thought was provocative.

Disgusted, Charlie turned back to the sink. He tried to hand Roheed a wet dish, but Roheed was still transfixed on the window. Charlie dropped the dish and it fell to the floor and shattered. He looked over to see what the heck Roheed was doing.

"Roheed."

"Um, what? I was just..."

Charlie saw that Roheed was staring at Florence. "Don't get your hopes up. That's Florence Comfortinn, socialite heiress to the Comfort Inn fortune."

"I didn't realize Comfort Inn had a fortune to speak of."

"It does, and she's the heiress to it. She's named after the first and most successful Comfort Inn Motel."

"Florence, Italy. How romantic."

"Actually Florence, Alabama."

"At any rate, she's exquisite."

"I heard she was dating Alabaster Sixx, son of the CEO of Motel 6. Could have been a rumor though."

"What is a diamond like her doing in this rough?"

"She's doing community service for something."

"Maybe it was for the theft of my heart."

Charlie patted him on the back. "Okay, buddy." They continued doing the dishes. Roheed was still awed. Charlie looked closely at a spatula. "This may sound strange, but does it look like someone has been cooking in here recently?"

CHAPTER 4

THE FRONT DOORS opened, and a flood of people walked into the Swim and Racquet Club with towels, sun hats and pool toys. Teens did increasingly daring flips off of the diving boards. Younger boys played an intense game of ping-pong. From his guard chair, Judas watched a couple ladies sunning themselves as a young girl sputtered in the three feet.

Bill patrolled the pool grounds, hugging women and kissing babies like a heavy metal politician. He air-guitared with the ping-pong playing pair and playfully guided the hips of an older woman playing shuffleboard. He left everyone he met with a rock-on devil's horns.

On the tennis courts, Florence briefed her tennis court workers. They were as young as legally possible with their signed work permits. For many of them it was their first job, and they were all chubby middle-schoolers with bad teeth or braces. Florence wore ridiculous designer sunglasses that were too big for her face, and she spoke in a disinterested, but surprisingly knowledgeable, voice.

"... and that is the line brush. It keeps the lines clean so our players can tell if a ball is out or whatever. Over there is the hose.

You can use it to spray, like, water and stuff. Since these are clay courts, they need to be kept moist at all times."

She bent over and picked up some clay and sifted it through her hands.

Judas stood with Matt Hedge, a goofy lifeguard with patchy facial hair, big teeth and a generic tattoo of a tribal sun. They watched Florence from behind a fence.

Judas leered. "I'd like to keep her moist at all times."

"That's what she said." Matt went for a high-five; Judas denied him.

"No, *I* just said that. But I tell you, she'll be mine by the end of the summer. I'm definitely at least going to can those hams."

"Totally dude-a-saurus."

"Seriously though, Florence is hot. I need a piece."

"Totally my bromosapien."

The inevitable high-five was then finally fived.

As Judas and Matt continued to ogle Florence, Jonathan threw out the first pitch of the first game of tennis baseball of the season. If you still don't know what tennis baseball is and can't glean what it could possibly be from the name, then first, I'm sorry that you have been deprived in your youth of a very terrific game, and second, you should take a look at your context clue sleuthery; then, I will tell you that tennis baseball is very much like America's favorite pastime, but with a racquet and tennis ball in place of the bat and baseball usually used.

Board-short-clad boys ran shirtless around the backfield of the club, blades of freshly cut grass clinging to their bare feet. That one kid was sitting in a deck chair, leg propped up, shirt on, complaining of a tweaked ankle when in actuality he didn't want to take his shirt off in front of the gaggle of girls that was forming to watch the young lads play. He would rather look like a wuss than risk being called ape-tits, or slopgut, or tons of fun, or flapjack titties, in front of his peers.

Jonathan's heart went out to the youngster—he too had had those awkward middle adolescent years that some do. So when Devon Wilkenshire, who had an eight-pack since birth and didn't understand body image issues, called to the chubby friend on the sideline, "Hey, fat ass, we need another player. Jiggle your double Ds on out here," Jonathan's pulse quickened, then slowed again with a zenlike calm.

He looked straight into Wilkenshire's soul and said, "Devon, your mom told me to let you know when it was eleven thirty so you could go use one of your medicated wipes. She said she knows your anus is all raw from diarrhea but that the wipes will help," and then he walked away, leaving the chips to fall where they may.

Wilkenshire sputtered that it wasn't true to the fellas, who were laughing their heads off, and his little fan club quickly dispersed, laughing and texting to each other about Devon's burning butthole. And for that young man who had been sidelined by shame, for that moment, his deck chair became a throne.

CHAPTER 5

THE SUN BEGAN to set on the Yellow County Community Swim and Racquet Club. Children were sunburned, mothers carried sleeping babies, and the lifeguards began to clean up. Bill waved to the regulars as they left. Judas picked up a pink swim noodle and pretended it was his giant foam weenie. He mock humped the air, then bumped Matt Hedge in the face a bunch of times, laughing. Florence apathetically hosed down the tennis courts without paying attention to where the water was spraying.

The first day had been a successful one. The opening day barbecue had gone off without a hitch—Mr. Jones had been a more than adequate grillsman. There were only two scraped knees the whole day, and they were on the same pair of legs. And the highlight of opening day, to some, was when The Hot Mom arrived. The middle school set didn't know how old she was (44), or what her name was (Jennifer Tribolini), or even whose mother she was (Timmy Tribolini, who spent most of the summer with his dad over in Brown County), but she was a legend. She walked the pool deck in her outdated bikini, tossing her too curly hair, unknowingly the fantasy of a flock of fourteen-year-olds. To them she was woman personified: curvaceous, exotic (well, tan at least), and experienced, and the pasty, flat-chested tween girls that were the boys' peers literally paled in comparison to The Hot Mom. Many a tall tale was told about her in the gazebo up by the satellite Har-Tru tennis courts in the southeast corner of the club compound. So yeah, when she sashayed into the YCCSRC that day, those young dudes were pumped, and to their delight she reclined in a chair all day, sunning.

• • •

At day's end, The Hot Mom pulled on a pair of high-waisted, stone-washed jeans that to everyone's surprise had come back into style, no one would have guessed that, and gathered her stuff into a tote. As she left she waved at Jonathan, who was spraying crud off of the deck chairs.

Bill approached him. "You heading out?

"Yep, really soon. I want to finish cleaning up first."

"Okay, see you dude." Bill turned to leave but stopped and turned back to Jonathan. "I'm worried."

"Don't worry, this nacho cheese always comes right off the metal with a little elbow grease. And I just got a whole tub of the stuff from the store." Jonathan smiled.

"Not about the deck chairs, Jonathan. Well, not just about the deck chairs, but where the deck chairs are."

"Gotcha, hose down the deck, too. Not a problem."

"No, Jon, the whole pool. I'm afraid the board might try something totally unrighteous.

• • •

Bill sat with other members of the pool board behind a long rectangular table in a dark back boardroom of the Yellow County Community Center. The only distinguishable one of them was June Summers, who looked like ten pounds of potatoes in an eight-pound bag, her fat face flushed red. For the rest of them, only their hands were visible—very Bond villainesque. Truth be told, they were only shrouded in darkness because that other light switch that controls half of the fluorescent lights was on the fritz again, and the maintenance man, Mr. John, hadn't gotten a chance to tinker with it, but still, the effect it created was ominous as heck.

Bill, in a black T-shirt with a graphic of a zombie in a nurse's uniform, sat on the opposite side of the table facing them defiantly as June ran the meeting.

"Next item on the agenda," she said, "do we turn the pool over to a management company or continue to be community run?"

Bill couldn't hold his tongue. "We provide jobs to nearly every teen in town. If it wasn't for our pool, those kids would be sexting and driving and doing bath salts for all we know. And they shouldn't do that until they're retired. All I want is to keep the family atmosphere where all the workers know your name and your mother's name."

"A management company will increase our profits exponentially," June rebutted.

The shrouded board murmured approval.

"How I see it..."—June began to daydream—"we'll have vending machines instead of that awful snack bar, rows of brightly lit automatons instead of the slack-jawed junkies that currently manage that grease trap. Wonderfully muscled professional lifeguards. And a decorative fountain right where the high dive is."

Bill grimaced. "That sounds like that godforsaken Brown Town Hall and Recreation."

June smiled. "Yes...yes, it does."

The shrouded board chuckled sinisterly.

June continued, "We'll raise membership fees and start catering to the folks from the city who actually have money and weed out the deadbeat community."

"No way," Bill shouted. "I will never turn the pool I love into a profit whore for the yuppie scum you're trying to attract."

"Oh, you will; one day you will. With how our finances are looking, you're going to have to sooner than you could imagine."

"Over my dead body. This meeting is adjourned." Bill stormed toward the door, knocking over a water cooler in the process. He put one leg up on the plastic bottle and launched into a killer air-guitar solo as the gallons of water glugged out.

• • •

Bill took a breath. "Hell's bells, I'm glad I got that off my chest."

Jonathan stared at Bill wide-eyed, but Bill continued. "Don't worry, as long as I'm alive and raising h-e-double diving boards those rat bastards aren't gonna touch us, trust me. I love this place too much not to fight for it." And with that he put on his headphones and pressed play on his cassette deck. He walked away playing the air guitar but paused to give Jonathan the "horns" over his shoulder. Jonathan waved politely and continued hosing down the deck.

Charlie was around the corner of the lifeguard office clocking out. He had heard the whole conversation. He stood, timecard in hand, brow furrowed.

CHAPTER 6

A FEW DAYS later, a storm blew in. The rain made little dimples in the pool water's surface, then it began to pour like buckets from heaven. Thunder bellowed, and Matt blew his whistle. Patrons scattered to get their belongings before they were soaked. The Hot Mom, who had been lying on her belly, bikini top undone to get sun on her tan line, got up with a start and held her still-unclasped top to her bosom as she rushed to gather her things.

Jonathan surveyed the darkening sky through the guard office window. He looked out and saw Bill holding a massive umbrella, from one of the wooden picnic tables, over the heads of a bunch of little kids. Jonathan got on the loudspeaker to make an announcement.

The speaker crackled with static as Jonathan cleared his throat and began, "Attention, testing, testing. One, two, three. One, two, three, testing one, testing two, testing three. Testing one, two, three. Attention testing. Attention one..."

Judas was reclining in a chair, watching *Rich B Words* on his smartphone. He paused the vid to yell in Jonathan's direction, "Bro! It works."

Jonathan, still over the loudspeaker, replied, "I just wanted to make sure. Okay, folks, I'm sorry, but we're going to have to close down for at least forty minutes after the last sighting of lightning or sound of thunder. That means we'll hopefully be opening back up at about three fifty."

Thunder roared.

"Three fifty one."

The thunder and lightning continued.

"Oh, never mind. Pool is closed. We'll reopen tomorrow."

The crowd of families began to leave, grumbling.

Florence ran around the courts, trying to gather tennis balls in a metal basket. The basket tipped, scattering the balls. Lightning flashed.

"Ugh, whatever." She ran toward the gate, her shoes making prints in the softening clay.

Charlie turned off some fuses in the box by the door as Roheed tied off the top of a large black garbage bag.

"May I have a ride home?" Roheed asked.

"Sure, your sister's got the car again?"

"My father has it this time."

Charlie checked his watch and said mostly to himself, "Whatever. I can't really go home yet anyway."

"What?"

Thunder crashed.

"Nothing. Here, meet me in the car. I have to put the cash in the safe," Charlie said as he picked up the cashbox and ran out into the rain.

Judas reclined in a chair in the guard office, sipping a beer. Charlie came in with the cashbox and unlocked the safe. Jonathan stepped in, soaking wet.

"Aren't you going to help clean up?" Jonathan asked.

Judas took a gulp of his brew. "Nope."

"We need your help. Bill is down there doing *your* job."

"I'm drinking beer, come on," he pointed to his can.

"Judas!" Jonathan's anger flared up for just a moment before he caught himself. "Go home, we'll manage without you."

"Stellar, bro." Judas put the lip of the beer can between his teeth as he put on his official Yellow County Community Swim and Racquet Club poncho, size XL, for Xtra Large rain protection.

As he exited the guard office, he lightly bumped shoulders with Jonathan. Jonathan just shook his head and walked out onto the pool deck.

He looked over the railing and saw that Bill was already down by the pool, moving chairs under an awning near the high diving board. His headphones were turned all the way up. Thunder and lightning boomed and zipped.

Jonathan yelled, "Bill, hey, Bill! Come on up here. The storm is getting too crazy." But his words were lost in the wind.

Lightning struck a tree branch near Jonathan and set it ablaze. Charlie exited the guard office to see what all the commotion was about. The tree branch fell. Jonathan dove and pushed Charlie out of the way as the wood splintered around them.

Another tree blew down and rocked the high dive. The board shuddered, and wire supports unsnapped from the structure.

Bill continued to rock out while his headphones blared.

A gust of wind blew the shuddering board completely off its support.

Charlie looked to Bill, then whipped his head to Jonathan, who had jumped up and taken off toward Bill. He ran down the steps from the guard office to the pool but was still too far to help, and he knew it.

Quietly, "No, Bill," escaped his lips.

Bill, unaware, slowly made his way across the pool deck. Jonathan looked away as the wind howled and the diving board toppled. Bill finally looked up and gasped, his eyes widening. The board fell on top of him, pinning his neck to the concrete, the snap not loud enough to be heard over the whooshing wind.

Jonathan ran through the sideways rain to Bill's side and heaved the massive board off of him.

He checked Bill's pulse. There was none.

Before the emotion hit him, Jonathan took two fingers and closed Bill's eyes. Then he took Bill's right hand in his and bent Bill's pointer and pinky fingers up into an eternal rock-on devil's horns position. He did the same with Bill's other hand and folded his arms over his chest. Heavy metal.

Charlie covered his mouth with his hand.

Jonathan then let himself break down as the storm continued around him, the blue fabric from what was left of the high diving board flapping in the wind like a truce flag in a war that was never meant to be won.

• • •

Dark clouds floated ominously above the dreary cemetery. A funeral procession band played "Stairway to Heaven" on horns in a deep, melancholy tone. A tuba blarted along.

Jonathan stood solemnly in a suit, with his lifeguard polo underneath a wrinkled dark jacket, his whistle dangling from around his neck on its usual red lanyard. Roheed wore a dark suit, Charlie a full-length black trench coat, and Florence was in a black designer dress and huge designer sunglasses. She texted casually.

Judas wore a black suit with a backward baseball cap and sipped a beer. Other patrons of the Swim and Racquet Club had shown up, too, along with a small moshpit's amount of old metal heads and Bill's now college aged grandson.

Jonathan was overcome with emotion before the eulogy was given. He ran from the funeral, through the cemetery and out the gate, and down residential streets until he reached the club.

He ran to the side of the pool and pulled off his suit pants, revealing that he was wearing his bathing suit underneath. As he started to tear up, he took a pair of goggles out of his suit jacket pocket. A single tear escaped before he could get them over his eyes. He stripped off his jacket and polo and dove into the pool, furiously swimming a lap across. He didn't pop his head out of the water to take a breath even once.

When he reached the other side, he got out and took off his goggles. They were full of tears. He sat, crying, on the pool's edge.

CHAPTER 7

JONATHAN SAT AT one end of a long table in a law office. The Pool Board was there, and even though the room was well lit, on the other side of the table, they sat shrouded in darkness, only June recognizable. This time, however, Mr. John couldn't be blamed. This time, the board was shrouded in whispers and deceit, and blackout curtains that kept the particular area where they were sitting quite dim.

At the head of the table, an older gent, parrotesque in appearance, Kenneth Strangleman, was perched reading from a folder through his thick glasses. The plaque in front of him showed his name and read *Estate Lawyer*.

June was impatient. "I've got to go pick up my kids. Can you please hurry up and tell us how the board will continue running the complex, and then we can all get out of here?"

Strangleman responded without looking up from the documents. "Hold on. I'm almost done with this paragraph... and...done. What now?"

June gestured to Jonathan. "Why is he here? He's just a lifeguard who, I might add, didn't do a very good job guarding Bill's life, did he?"

The shrouded board members chuckled vilely. Jonathan put his head down.

"Yes, this is very, very interesting. Very interesting indeed," Strangleman murmured.

"What?" June asked.

Strangleman held up a magazine, a random animal periodical he had in the folder on top of the documents. "Did you know that dolphins are one of the few animals other than humans known to mate for reasons other than reproduction?"

"Strangleman!" June yelled.

"Oh, right, the will. It seems that William has made Jonathan his heir."

Jonathan and June burst out at the same time, "What!?"

The board members rabbled.

Strangleman pounded a larger than average gavel on the table. "Be still. It's in Bill's will that Jonathan take over his fifty-one percent share of the Swim and Racquet Club."

"Fifty-one percent?" Jonathan said. "What are you talking about?"

Strangleman continued, "Bill won the majority share of the club in a high stakes game of canasta years ago. From me, actually. And I never forgave the bastard for it. I'm glad he's dead."

Strangleman spat on the floor but in the same breath said, "May he rest in peace. Anyway, you, Jonathan, are now the acting owner and caretaker of the pool, the snack bar, the tennis courts, and the tanning deck."

June put up her hand but did not wait to be called on. "What about the tetherball area?"

Strangleman replied, "Especially the tetherball area."

The shrouded board collectively gasped.

Jonathan piped up, "But look, Strangle Man."

"It's Strangleman."

"Sorry, Strangle Man. I don't know anything about running a pool."

Strangleman referred to a piece of paper in the folder. "It says in the personal letter from Bill that you have been doing exactly that for the past fifteen years."

June waved her hands as if swatting away the idea. "It doesn't matter. You won't own anything after this season. Add the current debt and now the cost of replacing the high dive, and what do you have?"

Jonathan answered glumly, "No more summers."

June said, "No, you idiot. It means that you won't be able to make the profit we need to keep the club community run. You'll be forced to hire a pool management company like *we've* always wanted. Stuff that in your sack, Samantha."

The board murmured excitedly.

Strangleman nodded. "I'm afraid what she's saying might be true, Samantha."

Jonathan began to rise from his chair. "My name isn't Samantha. And I agree. We will be run by a management company..."

June smiled for the first time in her life but immediately turned her frown right side up when Jonathan continued with, "Over my dead body!!"

Jonathan stormed toward the door, awkwardly knocking over the water cooler in defiance on his way out.

• • •

The pool was shut down. A sign hung out front that read, *Closed until further notice!!* (Not sure why there were exclamation points on that one, but hey, artistic license, right?)

Jonathan stood in the lifeguard corral, telling a lively story in front of Charlie, Roheed, Florence, Judas, Jill Bateman, and a handful of other staff members who sat at the umbrellaed wooden tables.

"And then I said 'over my dead body, Strangle Man.' And then I started to strangle Bill's estate lawyer, and I said 'who's the strangle man now?!' "

Roheed, amazed, said, "Wow."

Jonathan admitted, "The last part wasn't true, but still you get the gist of it."

"Right, so we're getting shut down," Judas remarked.

Charlie looked up with hope. "No we won't. Jonathan was just about to tell us his big plan, right?"

Jonathan looked back to Charlie. "My plan?"

"Yeah, the plan you've already devised to get us the money to cover our debts and get a new diving board. You already have that plan drawn up and ready right? And...go."

Jonathan shook his head. "I don't have a plan. I was hoping you guys were going to have some ideas."

No one did.

Charlie spoke after a few moments. "Roheed, how much have you made playing Internet poker?"

"Four thousand, eight hundred, thirty-six dollars, and sixty-nine cents."

Judas snickered. "Sixty-nine, nice."

"That'll at least cover the new board, right?" Charlie asked.

But Roheed continued, "That's what my earnings had been until yesterday when I blew it all on a huge bluff. My poker face did not translate via the Internet."

"Oh, okay. Well I don't have enough money for the first semester of film school yet, so I can't help." Charlie looked around.

"I would sell my body, but I'm saving it for marriage," Jill offered, then looked at Charlie and mouthed "to you."

"That's quite a range you've got, either prostitution or abstinence," Roheed smirked.

"I don't do anything halfway," Jill said, and looked at Charlie again. "Anything..." Then she made a circle with one hand and stuck out the pointer finger of the other, then poked the center of the circle with her pointer halfway, but quickly pulled it out of the circle, wagged it back and forth in a no-no fashion, then stuck the pointer all the way through the circle, in and out, several times.

Charlie, creeped out, nodded, "I get it."

"Dues just went up in my frat," Judas said. "I'm tapped like a keg on a Thursday afternoon. What about Regina Rich over there?" He pointed to Florence.

She stopped texting momentarily. "My assets are frozen until I finish my community service."

Judas whispered to Matt Hedge, "I'd like to warm her assets up."

Charlie, already knowing the answer, asked, "What did you get arrested for again?"

Florence went back to texting, uninterested. "DUI and indecent exposure when I stepped out of the car. I don't want to talk about it."

Judas honked. "I totally saw that episode of *Rich B Words*."

"Ew," Florence said, totally groadied out. "That was all in the editing anyway."

Charlie pulled the conversation back around. "How much does a diving board even cost?"

"I'm not sure. We bought that one..."—Jonathan gestured toward what was left of the old high dive, which was pretty much some metal rods and yellow caution tape that said "Cuidado" for some reason—"my first summer here for a couple hundred bucks."

"Back when you rode a dinosaur to work and gave Jesus a high-five that one time?" Judas chortled.

Only Matt laughed.

"I have a diving board guy coming," Jonathan said. "We open back up tomorrow, so go home and get some sleep."

Judas raised a single finger. "Are we still getting paid?"

"We'll see," Jonathan answered.

The employees dispersed. Judas could be overhead talking to Matt about how lame it would be if they weren't getting paid and how he would totally bail.

Roheed and Charlie walked out the front gate to Charlie's car.

"I kinda have to keep working here, pay or not," Charlie said.

Roheed glanced toward Florence, who was getting into her car. "And I will continue to work here as long as I am in sight of that masterpiece. She is my motivation for the intake of oxygen."

"You mean she's the air you breathe?"

Roheed nodded.

"That's cute," Charlie said. "You should find a way to tell her that that isn't creepy."

CHAPTER 8

CHARLIE WALKED INTO the kitchen of his parents' house wearing his trench coat. His mom and dad, Hilda and Art Heralds, sat eating at the dinner table.

Art beamed. "There's my hardworking man. Never thought I'd see the day."

Hilda gushed. "You are such a big little baby-man."

"Mom," Charlie grumbled.

"You want some dinner?" Hilda offered.

"No, I got something to eat already, in the city." Charlie tried to leave the kitchen as fast as possible.

Art was bothered by the trench. "Take off your coat and stay a while."

"Um." Charlie fiddled with the collar. "I need to fold it a certain way so it doesn't get wrinkled."

"Wasn't it too hot for it anyway? It was damned near ninety-eight degrees and rising downtown today, for Pete's sake!"

"It's chilly at my office, plus I need the pocket room."

"Ah, yes," Art mused. "The office, your grand internship that will propel you into the real world. Help you get a real job, a career if you will, and right downtown at the upstanding...where did you say it was again?"

Charlie thought fast. "The Washington DC Assemblage of Television and other Video Affairs Corporation...Commission."

Hilda, with a mouthful of food, said, "That's a mouthful," she swallowed, gesturing to the amount of food in her mouth, then continued. "And the name of your internship place is long, too."

"Sounds great to me," said Art. "Anything but that minimum-wage crap job you had at the pool the past few summers. Now you can start to save some money. Being in debt after college is an epidemic."

Charlie muttered under his breath, "Maybe if you planned to help pay for college..."

"What?" Art asked.

"I gotta take a shower," Charlie said. "I was sitting next to some guy on the Metro who smelled like pee *and* poop." He walked out of the room.

Art and Hilda shrugged and continued eating.

• • •

That night Charlie sat in his room at an old typewriter. Stacks of movies adorned every flat surface, and there were movie poster one-sheets on the wall. The interior decor was punctuated by the *Animaniacs* cartoon curtains on his window and a matching comforter on his bed—it was like a little kid's bedroom had been partially overhauled by a film enthusiast.

The page before him was blank except for *FADE IN:* written toward the top left corner. He stared out the window into the night.

Charlie hadn't meant to lie to his parents at first, but after he was turned down for a gig at the local news station, and he never heard back from that feature that was going into production for the summer downtown, and after even Popcorn Movies, the hellish movie rental chain that was on its way out, said thanks but no thanks for a summer position, what else was he to do but make up a fake internship and return to the easy job that paid crap that his dad hated?

He figured he was just killing time until the fall, when hopefully he would be attending Yellow State. So in the meantime he had bought a trench coat at the thrift store, watched a sewing tutorial on YouTube, and made a "young professional" disguise to wear for leaving and coming back to his parents' house.

And his parents weren't stupid, but it would never have entered their minds that their son had made up an internship, sewed sleeves, a collar, and pants into a coat, and was actually working at the local pool. I mean, who does that?

CHAPTER 9

THE NEXT MORNING Charlie sat in the same spot as before, sleeping. His head rested against his chest, and he breathed deeply.

Hilda called to him from downstairs. "Charlie! Rise and shine! Cockadoodle do, don't cockadoodle don't!"

Charlie woke and shuddered. He looked at the clock and groaned, then looked at the nearly blank page in front of him and groaned again, wanting to just cockadoodle die.

Charlie walked into the kitchen still rubbing the sleep out of his eyes. Art was reading the newspaper. With a cup of coffee in front of him, he looked over the top of the paper and eyed Charlie's feet suspiciously.

"You look very 'professional' today."

Charlie was wearing his trench coat. He looked down and saw that he was wearing his beat-up snack bar shoes.

"Oh, um, casual Friday?"

"It's Tuesday."

"Oh, yeah. It's the new rage at all the hip offices. Tuesday is the new Friday. Like how, uh, orange is the new black, or whatever..."

"I work in an office building."

"Well, tell your boss to get with the times."

"Mmm." Art wasn't buying it. "What is the name of the organization you're interning with again?"

"The, um, Washington DC Assembly of Television and other Video Associations Company...Commission."

"Where in the city is that?"

"Oh, you know, I just take the Metro to Foggy Bottom, then it's a quick jog over to...23rd street."

Art abandoned his paper. "Do you mean to tell me that you have an internship based out of the Lincoln Memorial?"

"Yes," Charlie began, then amended, "No. It's right behind it though. Similar addresses. We get their mail all the time. And vice versa."

"What kind of mail does the Lincoln Memorial receive?"

"Fan letters." Charlie reached. "The Penny Saver..."

Art just looked into Charlie's eyes.

Charlie continued, "Because...Lincoln is on the penny. Get it?"

Art picked his paper back up. "I think I'd like to meet your supervisor one day. One day soon. I'll see when I can get an extra hour off work to meet for lunch. The three of us."

Charlie gulped. "Okay, awesome."

• • •

Roheed watched Florence from the safe haven of the snack bar. He rested his face on his hand and stared dreamily as she walked the length of the court with a ball hopper, plunking the metal basket down on top of the neon orbs.

From the guard chair, Matt Hedge made eye contact across the pool to Judas, who was spinning his long red whistle lanyard on his finger. Simultaneously they blew their whistles, signifying adult swim. The kiddies groaned and slowly pulled their dripping bodies out of the pool, some running immediately to the locker room where they would stand under the hot showers, waiting until they heard that whistle again and they could run back to the pool to continue pruning their patooties; some running to the snack bar line, queuing up with their parents' cash to blow on Lemynheads and Cherry Klan.

A young lad of about five years old startled Roheed out of his daze. He was too short to reach the order window, so he simply put his hand up with a crinkled dollar and a mess of coins and dropped it all on the metal counter.

His high-pitched voice rose from below, "What can I get for this many?"

Roheed snapped back into snack bar mode. "You can purchase any number of permutations of candy, beverage, and/ or snack foods with that amount."

The young lad looked up at Roheed blankly. "I want something tasty."

So Roheed began telling him, in great detail, the numerous combinations of junk food he could buy with a dollar and eighty-three cents, much to the dismay of the line of kids behind him.

Meanwhile, Charlie sat at a small table in the back of the snack bar, well, less of a table, and more of a board that was nailed to two walls in a back corner. Empty food trays and rolls of coins cluttered his writing space as he sat with a blank notebook in front of him. He tapped on the page with his pen, a blue Bic Round Stic he had the habit of carrying in his left front pocket wherever he went.

Jill Bateman padded over to Charlie and stood too close.

"Whatcha writin'?"

Charlie, guarded, said, "I'm just trying to think of some ideas."

"What for?"

"A movie or a short story or something. Anything really."

"I write song lyrics."

"Are you in a band or something?"

"No."

Charlie should have stopped there, but his curiosity was twanged like a banjo at a yard sale. "Oh, it's like a solo project? What instruments do you play?"

"I don't play any."

"So you just write the lyrics? No music?"

"Nope, but they're really good. They're old school, like Blink-182."

Charlie nodded. He understood now. "Oh, cool. You'll have to show them to me sometime."

He went back to tapping his pen—think, think, think—like a sad food-service-business version of Winnie the Pooh.

But Jill wasn't finished chatting yet. "You mentioned film school, right?"

"Did I? Yeah, I guess. I'm going to go for screenwriting."

"What are you going to do with that?"

Charlie, sadly, said, "Probably nothing."

"You should write like, *The Hangover*."

"I think that's already been written."

"They say every story has already been written." She said.

She had a point.

She continued. "My mom said that when I go to college it's going to be right here in the community. I'm going to the community college."

Charlie nodded. "That's really convenient. Sounds really great."

Jill made her move. "I'll still be close to you." She moved one of her cheeks to sit on Charlie's thigh.

Charlie scooted his stool away quickly. "Jill, we've been over this. You're fourteen."

Jill pouted. "And three-quarters..."

Roheed called from the front, "Charlie! Board member!"

Charlie dashed into action. He grabbed a hat and put it on as he threw a hat to Roheed for him to cover his curly black locks. Roheed ushered a teenaged worker into the back of the bar, out of sight where he couldn't visually violate any health code regulations. Jill just watched, frozen.

Charlie grabbed Jill by the shoulders. "This isn't a drill. We have to pretend this place is sanitary."

She tied her hair back. Charlie turned off the stereo. June, the board member, walked up to the window. Expensive sunglasses covered her eyes but she tilted them down and looked right past Roheed. "Scoot your boot, Kumar. Charlie, how are things?"

Charlie, a little bead of sweat on his brow, replied, "Great. Everything is fine."

"Great or fine?"

"Great."

"Are you being an acceptable manager?"

Charlie said quietly, "I don't think I could be much worse

than the last guy you hired."

June folded her flabby arms across her chest. "You aren't doing so great yourself, buckaroo. All those health code violations really hurt us last year."

Charlie tried to stay calm. "With all due respect, ma'am, the one and only violation we got was for the microwave that the board wouldn't replace. After the front screen fell off, we were probably exposed to dangerous waves of—"

"Beside the point," June interrupted. "You should have duct taped it or something. You better watch your ass now that Bill's gone."

Charlie tried to start, "You—"

"Irrelevant," June shut him down. "I want to make an order. I am on a very strict diet so I'll have a veggie burger and a salad."

Roheed piped up, "A lot of our usual items were out of stock when we went on our last run."

"Extraneous information. I'll change my order to one double cheeseburger and freedom fries with cheese. And make it fast."

Charlie scribbled the order down on a nearby Post-It. "OK."

"And I want cheese from that pot." June pointed to a filthy crock pot o' nacho cheese. Hardened orange goo was stuck around the rim of the lid. "And you better believe I want my buns toasted."

Roheed scurried to the back of the snack bar to grab the fixins. He tossed two frozen patties on the grill, and they began to sizzle.

CHAPTER 10

FOR THE FIRST weeks following Bill's death, few patrons populated the reopened pool grounds. This didn't bode well for the morale of the crew, but they reconciled that people were probably on family vacations and the weather wasn't great, so... you know, whatever.

And they continued lying to themselves on Hot Dog Night, usually a huge event, where Charlie would sweat it out in the snack shack, grilling dogs and toasting buns for hours as the pool stayed open late, and kids could bring their boogie boards and alligator floats and ride them in the pool. The highlight of the night was a trio of black truck tire inner tubes that were brought out of the back storage shed and let loose in the water. Middle-schoolers would spend the entire four hours crowding around the tube, jockeying for position, hoisting themselves up, then getting knocked off by the next king of the float. The following morning they would wake up with chafed nips from the harsh rubber that they had so gladly rubbed their tender chests against the night before.

But on this Hot Dog Night the truck tires floated listlessly, bumping into the sides of the pool like the most boring game of

Pong you've ever seen. Charlie made maybe a dozen hot dogs, and most of those were for a dad who was there chaperoning his tween daughter.

And the last straw, when they knew they were screwed, was illustrated by the poor attendance at Ruby's early morning Senior Swim & Sweat. Ruby, who by all accounts wasn't really in great shape herself, led a six a.m. aerobics class in the three feet. It was always hopping with geriatric fitness enthusiasts wearing floppy hats and eye-surgery grade sunglasses, lifting foam dumbbells above their heads and listening to "Gangnam Style" as they felt the burn.

So even though Jonathan had only planned to look into possibly finding out how to go about getting a new high dive, he actually had to do some legwork to get a diving board specialist over to the YCCSRC, because that would solve all their problems, he thought.

• • •

Jonathan stood next to the broken high dive with a tough looking gal with *Chris* stitched onto the breast of her polo shirt, size S, to show off her size L guns. On the back of the shirt it read *The Diving Broad: More Splash, Less Cash* and a phone number with a MoCo area code.

"Chris" worked on a mouthful of chewing tobacco as they assessed the board sitch'.

"Board is spelled wrong on your shirt there," Jonathan pointed out.

"No it's not. It's broad," Chris said as she spit a mouthful of black tobacco juice into the pool.

Jonathan looked at the floating phlegm for a second, then he gestured toward the diving board. "What do you think it'll cost to replace her...it?"

"Well"—Chris loogied into the water—"I think you could be doing double-gainers this very afternoon for the low, low price of five G's."

"Five thousand dollars? Don't you have anything cheaper?"

"We do, but how many more lives do you want your diving board to take?"

Jonathan winced. "We just aren't making that kind of money

right now. Membership numbers are at an all-time low. It seems the whole 'guy dying on the premises' thing is scaring people away."

Jonathan looked away from Chris and had a moment. "I miss him."

Chris broke the moment as she spit a glob of goo into the pool. "They'll be dying to get *on* the premises with the DiveMaster9000 state-of-the-art diving board system."

Jonathan sighed. "Okay, I'll give you a call once we round up the money."

Chris pointed to the back of her shirt with two thumbs as she indicated the company phone number. Her hands were directly on top of two screenprinted-on hands already in the logo.

"Just ask for Chris," she said.

"Is that short for Christine or something?"

"No."

"Crystal?"

"No."

"Christen?"

"Nope."

"Chrysanthemum?"

Chris shook her head and donated a final wad of chew to the water of the YCC pool as she walked away.

CHAPTER 11

TO STOCK THE snack bar, a manager would have to drive to the nearby exceptional wholesale bulk food club. They would ride a flatbed cart down the aisles, picking up cans of ketchup, boxes of candy, and vats of oil that, when heated, cooked most things to a crispy, artery-tightening, brown, delicious color and texture. If the truck tires bouncing around the empty pool were like a terrible Pong, then the stacking of snack bar necessities on the flatbed was its Tetris-esque counterpart.

Usually Charlie had to restock once or twice a week, but it had been a full fortnight since he re-upped. They just weren't doing business since Bill died.

Charlie and Roheed stood at the snack bar window, surveying the nearly empty pool grounds. A flag waved at half-mast. Judas walked by the window.

Charlie called out to him, "Hey, Rude Jude."

"'Sup?"

"Did you put the flag at half-mast for Bill's death?

"Who's Bill?"

"He owned the pool."

Judas looked back at Charlie blankly.

"He just died."

Still nothing.

"You were at his funeral."

A lightbulb. "Oh, that guy? I was just there for the free beer."

"You brought your own beer," Charlie replied. "Anyway, Jonathan will really appreciate the gesture."

"What gesture?" Judas asked. "My arms got tired while I was hoisting it. My 'ceps are still sore from a killer set of curls I knocked out last night."

Charlie shook his head in disbelief. Florence approached them with a sheet of paper. Roheed immediately perked up. Unfortunately, so did Judas.

"Hey, babe," he said.

Florence was disgusted by both of them so she directed her attention toward Charlie, which he thought was a good thing, until he further analyzed it and came to the conclusion that she thought of him as a sexless automaton, thus nonthreatening. "Here's the deal: I wouldn't normally talk to you, like, ever, but have you seen this?"

Charlie gave the sheet a quick once over. "The Tri-County Relay Race sign-up? Sure."

"The prize money could buy a new diving board. First place is ten thousand dollars and a frozen margarita machine."

"You're right," Roheed added. "Plus it's being held here at Yellow County Community this year. The revenue could make up for our past couple years' losses."

"That too, I guess," Florence unenthusiastically responded.

"Why do you care?" Charlie asked.

"If the pool gets shut down, I'll have to finish my community service restocking clothes at a thrift store...ew."

"I hate to burst your bubble, but even if we did make enough on ticket sales and concessions to pay our debts, we still wouldn't win the prize money, and the safety inspector would still shut us down for having a dangerous board."

"Why?"

"The team over at Brown Town always wins. They're run by a management company, so technically they can bring in swimmers from any of their conglomerates in the Tri-County area. I swear they hire ringers and give them menial jobs just so they can swim."

"Whatever, bro," Judas contended. "I have friends that work at Brown Town. It's totally legit."

"Brown Town?" Florence didn't like the sound of that at all.

"You've never heard of the Brown Town Hall and Recreation Relay Race Team?" Charlie asked, already knowing the answer. "The BTH and Triple RT?"

"No." Florence acted like Charlie had just asked if she'd ever eaten some doo-doo.

"A few years ago, Jonathan wanted to beat them so bad he did some reconnaissance on them. There's a tape in the office."

Minutes later, Charlie, Florence, Roheed and Judas piled into the guard office. Judas pressed *eject* on a small TV/ VCR combo, and OMG, a CPR training tape popped out. Charlie handed Judas an unlabeled tape. Judas put in the tape and pressed play.

On the TV screen there was a moment or two of snow, and then a shaky home video camera image emerged and showed, sometimes obscured by out-of-focus bush branches, the Brown Town Hall and Recreation state-of-the-art pool facility.

There were diving boards of varying heights and fountains and large floating foam lily pads (for the kiddies). The lifeguards were chiseled male model types and sexy youngish girls with short shorts that said "Guard" on the butt. There was a row of vending machines and a microwave in lieu of a snack bar.

"That place is awesome," Judas said, eyes glued to the monitor. "Look at those chicks."

Florence quit texting for the moment to focus her attention on the video. "This looks like a lame version of a country club I got kicked out of once for wearing a thong-brero." Roheed looked at her with confusion. Florence rolled her eyes. "A thong/sombrero hybrid, duh."

"You should see it on the weekend," Charlie said. "People from DC swarming all over the place, a different set of lifeguards every day, and the only food you can get is high-priced microwaveable diet meals and quinoa. It's so impersonal."

"Yeah, how are they supposed to get food poisoning?" Judas sneered.

The camera panned along the pool, surveying the lap lanes.

A set of twins, a boy and girl (but you could hardly tell because of their beautiful Michael Pitt from *Funny Games* haircuts) were in one lane. They both looked to be in their late teens, and they wore matching brown swimsuits. They treaded water facing each other with their arms completely out of the pool.

"That's Channan and Shannon Twinsley," Charlie explained.

"Twins that are both named Shannon?" Florence guessed she had heard of stranger.

"No, Channan and Shannon. Pronounced the same, spelled differently."

"Homophones," Roheed added.

The twins got out of the water and hugged.

"And they're creepily close," Charlie said.

"Weird." Florence was indeed creeped.

Channan stretched Shannon's legs for her as a mysterious woman watched in the background.

Charlie pointed at the screen. "That looks like June. Pause it."

Roheed paused the tape, but since it was a crappy VHS, they couldn't make out any of the mysterious woman's features. She was just a blurry smudge.

"Inconclusive, bro," was Judas's verdict.

Roheed hit *play* and the camera panned over to the next lane, where a young man was swimming. He blazed through a lap in record time and got out at the other end of the pool, not even breathing hard.

He was clad in only a brown brief-cut bathing suit. He looked remarkably like Olympic Gold Medalist Michael Phelps but with a thick, dark mustache.

The camera zoomed in on his rippling six-pack.

"That's Carmichael Schmelps, the fastest swimmer in the Tri-County area," Charlie said.

"Carmichael Schmelps?" said Florence. "He looks an awful lot like Olympic Gold Medalist Michael Phelps. Well, except for that thick, dark mustache, of course."

Judas responded, defensively, "He's definitely not though. Brown Town can prove it. They've got his birth certificate and everything. Plus look at that thick, dark mustache you mentioned!"

Charlie and Roheed looked at Judas.

"Just saying is all," he added quietly.

The camera panned over again to the next lap lane. A fin cut through the cool blue water, making little ripples on either side of it.

"What is that?" Florence asked.

A woman reached the end of her lap lane and got out of the pool. She had a broad, flat face, a manly body, and a fin-shaped protuberance on her back covered by her brown one-piece swimsuit.

Again, Charlie had the answer. "That is Susan Hark. She underwent experimental surgery that put shark cartilage into her back to help stabilize her as she swims."

"She has a dorsal fin," Roheed clarified.

Florence was sort of getting into it. "That can't be legal!"

"The official Tri-County Relay Race rules state that anyone with corrective surgery is still allowed to compete," Charlie explained.

"Adding a dorsal fin is corrective surgery?"

"She has scoliosis."

The camera zoomed out, and all four of the Brown Town team members swam furiously down their lap lanes. Overheard on the tape's audio track Jonathan said, "Crap, they're fast."

Jonathan walked into the guard office and saw what they were watching; he whistled, "Crap, they're fast. What are you guys doing?"

"Surveying the enemy in their natural habitat so we can better understand them," Roheed answered.

"We're going to get creamed again this year," Jonathan stated.

"I want to try to win," Florence said. "I don't want to sort clothes that people died in for the rest of my community service."

Roheed saw her vigor and found himself saying, "I would like to join the team as well."

Florence gave Roheed a look that wasn't purely one of disgust for the first time.

Judas noticed. "Yeah, I'll join, too."

"Charlie?" Jonathan said.

"No thanks. I don't swim. I wish you the best though."

"I guess that just leaves me," Jonathan supposed. "I'll practice with you guys, but only because we're probably going to lose the pool. I'll get in all the lap swimming I can before they give me the boot...plus our usual anchor, Matt Hedge, has a hernia."

"How'd that happen?" Charlie asked.

(Earlier that day, Matt Hedge had sat on the can in his bathroom. In the midst of a very satisfying bowel movement, he sneezed. His face wrenched in pain.)

Standing proudly was the newly formed YCCSRC Relay Race Team...and Charlie.

Jonathan stretched out his hand. "Let's start training tomorrow. I know I'm free. Maybe we can save this pool yet. Hands in."

Charlie shrugged and put his hand in the middle. "Good luck."

Florence put her hand kind of in the circle but not close enough to touch the others. "Don't touch my hand."

Roheed put his fingers into the *live long and prosper* symbol and put it on the hand pile.

Judas, not to be outdone, added a Dane Cook "superfinger" to the mix.

Jonathan puffed up his chest. "I think that if Bill hadn't died in that freak accident, he'd be here with us, smiling. Who knows, maybe Ghost Bill *is* here with us right now, screaming out in a futile effort to warn us that this is going to be a huge waste of time because as a ghost he has privilege to see the future, yet no power to communicate with the living. Or maybe he's scheming on chicks in the women's locker room because that's what he always used to say he was gonna do when he died. At any rate, for Bill."

They all, even Florence, raised their hands in the air and said, "For Bill!"

Judas's hand grazed Florence's breast in the downswing. She glared at him. He put up his hands in defense. "Totally an accident."

CHAPTER 12

IT WAS ABOUT that time of the Earth's rotation when you could not quite be sure if it was very late at night or very early in the morning, and much like the glass half-full/ half-empty conundrum, no one really gave two shakes of a lamb's tail.

The combination lock on the YCCSRC's front gate latch was unlocked as Roheed slipped quietly through to the pool grounds. He reached the pool's edge and slipped off his shirt, revealing a very skinny body and maybe three chest hairs if we're being generous here. He took off his shoes and dipped a toe in the water. He was in the deep end near the fallen high dive, which was inadvertently serving as a monument to the club that used to exist when Bill was still around.

Roheed tried to cautiously lower himself into the water but slipped and fell all the way in, making a huge splash.

He bobbed to the surface and thrashed wildly. He went back under and swallowed water; his wet hair clung to his face and covered his eyes.

In the guard office, Jonathan bolted upright in the cot that served as his makeshift bed. "Danger!!" he said as he kicked off the sheet and ran out the door.

Yep, Jonathan lived secretly at the pool. In his tenure there, this was not the first time he was awoken in the middle of the night by unexpected guests. Usually it was teens, breaking into the pool for a drunken night swim. One of them would be an employee who knew the combo for the tennis gate, and they would all sneak in 40s of OE, or neon-colored Mad Dogs, or poorly mixed cocktails from their parents' liquor cabinets. And Jonathan would have to hide under his cot, because he couldn't expose his secret.

But this time was different. Jonathan ran to the pool deck. Roheed was barely keeping his head above water long enough to gasp some air.

"Hang on, little buddy!" Jonathan cried as he ran down the stairs. He tore off his polo and dove into the water. He grabbed Roheed around the chest and swam him to safety, hoisting his small frame out of the water and onto the pool deck.

Roheed coughed up a mouthful of water immediately.

Jonathan looked down at him warmly. "You're going to be fine."

After Roheed stopped shivering, Jonathan sat on a metal folding chair, and Roheed sat on a cot with a towel draped over him wearing an official YCCSRC hoodie, size L, which fit Roheed like a size XXL, and it was providing him an XXL amount of warmth, too.

"How did you arrive so quickly?" Roheed was confused but grateful.

"I, uh, have super powers."

"Were you sleeping in the guard office?"

"Of course not. That's crazy talk. You're a crazy person."

"Have you been living in the guard office and keeping it a secret?"

"That's crazy. You are the silliest little guy."

"Then what's this?" Roheed pulled an issue of *Swimgirl* magazine from underneath the pillow on the cot. On the cover was a sexy girl in a one-piece bathing suit, a swim cap and a nose plug. The headline read, "You won't believe how Kelly practices her *laps*."

"Okay, okay, put that away. I live here. Happy?"

"Why?"

"I don't want to talk about it."

Roheed picked up the *Swimgirl* again, flipped to a random page, and began reading, "Kelly says 'Divers that can splash me with their big cannonballs make me wet.'"

"Stop, alright. I'll make a long story medium-length."

"I have time."

So Jonathan began.

• • •

The Yellow County Community Swim and Racquet Club looked pretty similar in the '80s: guard office, snack bar, tennis courts. But the girls wore legwarmers with their bathing suits, dudes dressed *Miami Vice* style, black guys had gold chains around their necks and shell-toed shoes. There were mustaches aplenty.

Young Jonathan spent a lot of time at the pool with his real dad. They splashed each other in the shallow end and ate ice cream sandwiches. Jonathan would marvel when his dad would do a one-and-a-half off of the high dive. They had the best times.

When he was about fifteen, Jonathan became a lifeguard. He patrolled the pool compound twirling his whistle one way until the red lanyard wrapped all the way around his pointer finger, then twirled it back the other way for the same result. Girls watched him out of the corners of their eyes, but he would always walk right past them to hang with his dad, who would just be coming from his night shift. They'd share an order of mozzarella sticks—Jonathan's breakfast and his dad's dinner due to their opposite schedules.

Only a couple years later, Jonathan's dad would die in an industrial laundry press machine, The Mangler. Jonathan wept as he leaned on the closed casket at the funeral. Then, Jonathan was the man of the house for approximately one week, the time it took for his mom to meet his dad's co-worker, Rick, who dropped by to pay his respects and see if she wanted to maybe share his twelve-pack of beer that he had brought or something.

On his eighteenth birthday, Jonathan moved out of the house as Rick moved in. Having nowhere else to go, or at least nowhere else he wanted to go, he snuck into the YCCSRC's guard office.

He set his box of belongings in the corner, thinking it was going to be a temporary solution, but days turned into weeks, weeks turned into months, and that box was still in the exact same place near the cot in the guard office as Jonathan told Roheed his life story.

Jonathan gestured to the club. "This was the only place that felt like home once my dad was gone."

"A psychological projection of emotions for your father onto a physical place. Interesting."

Jonathan looked at Roheed blankly.

"Never mind," Roheed said.

"Why were you here? Did you come here just to drown, or...?"

"Alas, my strict upbringing and even stricter study habits have prevented me from learning how to swim. Now I must teach myself the art in order to participate in the relay race and woo my beloved."

Jonathan said hesitantly, "Judas?"

"No, you moron. Florence."

"Ahh, she's kind of a b-word though."

"I see her inner beauty shining through like a beacon. A lighthouse to my ship lost at sea."

"Oh, alright. Well let's make a deal. You keep my secret—"

"I'm listening."

"And I'll teach you how to swim. I mean, I used to coach the six and under swim team, and they were mostly stupid idiots."

"Agreed. Shall we meet after the pool closes as to not arouse suspicion?"

"Yeah, and don't come to our real practices for a while. I don't want you to look stupid in front of Florence, because like I said, she's kind of a b-word."

Roheed shrugged and nodded.

"Now get out of here," Jonathan said. "I need my beauty sleep."

Roheed got up to leave.

Jonathan moved to the cot and draped Roheed's towel over the chair.

Roheed was almost out the door when he stopped and turned around. "Jonathan?"

"Yeah?"

"Thanks."

Roheed left the guard office. There was a soft clank when he closed the front gate. Jonathan fluffed up his pillow and lay back. He took out a picture of himself and Bill where he was smiling wide for the camera and Bill was slightly confused and wearing his headphones but being a good sport nonetheless and throwing up a rock-on devil's horns.

The rest of the night, Jonathan slept peacefully, the picture rising and falling with his chest.

CHAPTER 13

EARLY THAT MORNING, before the pool opened and just after the sun had rubbed his sleepy eyes and decided that he guessed he'd better rise again that morning, after all, there's no snooze button for a star, Jonathan showered in the men's locker room, wearing his faded red lifeguard shorts and lanyarded whistle.

The shower was an open area with four communal showerheads. Jonathan liked to stand in the middle with all four pointed at him spraying steaming hot water, but that day he modestly used just the one.

He pulled his shorts away from his body with his thumb, then dripped some soap to his nether region, allowing the sudsy water to run down into his shorts.

In the snack bar he made himself breakfast. He licked a red, white and blue Rocket Pop as he flipped a burger on the grill. He wore his favorite apron, the one that said, *Kiss the Cook... Please!!!?!*

He ate his breakfast at one of the picnic tables in the outdoor dining area. He looked out over the pool, and all was good.

And as the day wore on, it went better than the last. More

moms were showing up for lap swim, and more old gents ambled in and sat at the back picnic tables, playing euchre or gin rummy, and then people started coming to swim. It turned out to be a hot day, and maybe some thought that a good way to honor Bill's memory was to go hang at the pool that he had made so special for them.

A lot of people were heading to the grill, too. Charlie worked feverishly there, cooking hamburgers and hot dogs and a chicken quesadilla that some brash customer ordered. Chicken quesadillas were the worst, because you had to cook the chicken, cut it up, lay it on a tortilla, cover the meat with cheese, then cook the tortilla on the grill. The hardest part was flipping the thing, because if you waited too long, the tortilla would burn, but if you didn't wait long enough, you would flip the quesadilla and all of the cheese would spill out on the grill...there was a small window on those gosh-darned things. Smoke poured off of the hot meat and into Charlie's eyes. He wiped away tears and sweat.

There were dozens of orders that needed to be filled scrawled on Post-It notes and clipped to a strip of wood that ran above the order window. To make matters worse, someone had bought the Post-Its where the sticky strip alternated top and bottom in an infuriating accordion style instead of just being sticky all at the top like the traditional strips. As Charlie cooked away and struggled with the Post-Its, Roheed diligently prepared the drinks and sides and arranged them with the cooked meat in buns on trays.

Jill idled by the order window. A customer approached with two cardboard boats of sad-looking fried cheese.

"I just received two orders of mozzarella sticks..."

Jill, uninterested, said, "Yeah?"

"... that are completely frozen in the middle." He banged a frozen stick against the metal counter.

"Sucks."

"And my Sloppy Joe was only an Unkempt Joe. I want my Joe really disheveled. I need more Joe sauce."

Jill snickered.

Charlie stuck his head out the window. "We'll refund your money and replace those. I guess whoever was working the fryer wasn't paying attention." He glared at Jill.

Jill batted her eyes.

In the grease fryer bubbled a large cluster of food that was forming a huge mozzarella-stick-chicken-tender-filet-of-fish hybrid.

Charlie sighed and told the customer, "I'll put my best man on it. We'll call you in five."

The customer skulked off and said to himself, "But I'm hungry now."

Charlie called to Roheed, "You heard all that?"

Roheed popped his head from around the back corner, already balancing a handful of mozzarella sticks like a breaded, white cheese cheerleader pyramid. "I'm on it!"

Charlie's phone rang. It was his dad, Art, calling. He put down his burger flippin' spatula and headed toward the back of the bar, passing Roheed as he skittered to the front. He turned to watch Roheed deftly multitask.

Jill was carrying a tray of condiments, not paying attention to where she was going. She bumped into Charlie, smearing ketchup and mustard onto his crotch.

Jill smiled. "Woopsies."

Charlie answered the phone anyway, dabbing at his pants with a wet paper towel. "Hello?"

"Hey, there," Art said. "I was wondering if we could do that lunch soon."

"How soon?"

"How about in an hour at Ben's?"

"I already have lunch plans."

"Cancel them."

"I don't think my mentor is around."

"He left you unsupervised? Balderdash. I expect you outside Ben's with your mentor in an hour."

"I really don't think—"

Art clicked off.

Charlie looked around, assessing the situation.

Roheed appeared. "Anything the matter?"

"If the health inspector comes, don't let him or her in. You're the grillmaster now. Wear this apron with honor." Charlie handed Roheed the apron. It read *Hot Meat Patrol*.

Roheed regarded it with reverence.

Charlie dashed out the door.

Roheed called after him, "I will not let you down...," and added a "sir!" for good measure.

• • •

Charlie rushed past the guard office, where Jonathan was examining some pool water samples. Jonathan looked up and saw Charlie's distress.

"Charlie!"

Charlie poked his head into the office. "Yeah?"

"What's the matter? You need some help?"

"No. Kind of. Maybe."

"What can I do to help you?"

"Have you ever acted before?"

"I played charades once with my dad in middle school."

"I have a spare outfit in my trunk," Charlie said to Jonathan, then continued to himself, "That means I'm in the trench coat."

"Okay..."

Jonathan called out the guard office window, "Judas, you're head operator in charge."

"Righteous!" Judas waited for Jonathan to be just out of sight before he opened a beer and began to chug it.

A very fair-skinned portly young man waddled by.

Judas tweeted his whistle at the lad. "Get a tan!"

• • •

Art stood outside Ben's. He looked at his watch impatiently, then had to look at it again because he realized that he hadn't registered what time it was when he had looked the first time.

Charlie and Jonathan arrived, Charlie in his trench coat cover-up and Jonathan in Charlie's other pair of business clothes that fit him rather snugly, size M for the medium amount of deception this costume would warrant.

Charlie whispered to Jonathan, "Be cool."

Art extended his hand to Jonathan. "Hello, I'm Arthur Heralds, Charlie's father."

"Hi, Jonathan Poole, Charlie's manager."

"He means mentor," Charlie said to Art and turned to Jonathan with a glare. "Don't you, Mr. Poole?"

Jonathan, graciously, said, "Of course." Jonathan's whistle dangled from the red lanyard around his neck.

Art eyed it. "Is that a whistle?"

"Why, yes." Jonathan fingered the scuffed metal. "Yes, it is."

Charlie forced a laugh. "It can get pretty crazy in the office. Sometimes Mr. Poole here has to blow it to make sure we're staying on task."

"And no running," Jonathan added. "We're a very safety conscious atmosphere."

Art gestured to the restaurant. "Why don't we go in? They have the best burgers."

"Oh, man," Jonathan said glumly. "That's what I had for breakfast."

Art looked at Charlie. Charlie said knowingly, "Atkins Diet."

Art rolled his eyes. "I guess that would explain why someone smells like a grill."

"I don't know anything about that..." Charlie darted into the restaurant.

Soon, Art, Jonathan, and Charlie were sitting and chowing down.

Art grilled Jonathan like a Yellow County Snack Bar All-American beef hamburger sandwich patty. "How long have you been doing what you do?"

"A long time. Crazy long."

"And what is it exactly that you do at the um, Commission?"

Jonathan nervously reached for his glass of water and spilled it directly on his crotch. Charlie grabbed his napkin, reached for Jonathan's lap, then thought better of it and just handed the napkin to him.

"It's okay, guys. I have my bathing suit on underneath."

Charlie laughed nervously. "Office joke, long story. Too long to tell."

"Anyway, Jonathan, how has Charlie been doing this summer?"

"We haven't gotten any complaints yet."

"That's good. I wouldn't want my boy embarrassing himself. Do you know what his last job was?"

"Umm..."

"He worked in a snack bar. Can you believe it? A snack bar.

How low can you get?"

"At least he wasn't a lifeguard, right?" Jonathan chuckled.

Art nodded and took a bite of his burger. "That's true."

Charlie received a text from Roheed: *ETA?*

Back at the pool, Roheed waited for a return text from Charlie. Within seconds, it came: *ASAP, hold down the fort.*

Roheed put the phone in his pocket and surveyed the snack bar. Jill looked up guiltily from the three-basin sink—it was overflowing with sudsy water. Roheed looked out the window. June was talking to a patron. She laughed at something the patron said and started to walk toward the snack bar. As soon as she turned away from the patron her fake smile retreated from her mug, which had been described by many as a "resting B word face." Her features, left to their own devices, yearned to frown, clench and seethe.

Roheed texted back to Charlie: *Hurry.*

Back at the restaurant, Art was "peeping the scene" as they say and asked Charlie if he was, "Talking to someone important?"

"No, just Roheed...from accounting, such a kidder."

"When can I get the grand tour?"

Charlie and Jonathan exchanged worried glances. Charlie spoke. "At the office? No, they're doing a lot of renovations right now. Lots of asbestos, you know."

Jonathan piped up, "But they're getting rid of it 'as-best-os' they can!"

"Plus the air conditioning has been acting up. It's just not comfortable to be there right now."

"But you've been wearing that huge trench coat every day."

"Yeah, too much AC is the problem. I know how you hate being cold."

Charlie got another text: *June here, trying to stall...*

Back at the pool, June was standing at the snack bar window.

"... I believe he went down to dry storage to get some twenty-ounce cups," Roheed told her.

"I hope that is the case, Aladdin. I don't like to think about what I would have to do if I caught you running this place without a state-licensed food handler."

"Yes, ma'am. No, definitely twenty-ounce cups. They're very popular, you see, because the average human bladder can hold thirteen ounces of liquid, so after you fill up and urinate you can be like, oh, good, another...seven... ounces... for um, later."

June wasn't thoroughly convinced of the twenty-ounce cup's rabid popularity. "I think I better come in and take a look..."

The patron that June had been talking to called out to her, "June! June, come watch little Padme. She can stand in the four feet now."

June turned to the woman, all smiles. "Be right there, honey."

She turned back to Roheed, all business. "Charlie better be back with those cups by the time I'm done watching this little brat stand in the shallow end."

Meanwhile at the restaurant, Charlie had just finished a dissertation on why Art should never and could never visit the office where he and Jonathan worked.

"I get it," Art said. "Well, what's the website at least? I'd just really like to know more about what you've been doing with your summer."

"Just drop it, okay? You're meeting Jonathan right now. What more proof do you need? Come on!"

Art's face crinkled. Charlie softened. "What I mean is...I'm really busy most days, and I just don't want to interrupt our work flow."

Jonathan nodded, his mouth full with his last bite of burger. "Definitely."

"In fact, we need to be getting back." Charlie stood and left some money on the table. He motioned for Jonathan to follow.

Art sat, stunned, and then he noticed the money that Charlie left behind. There was a smudgy ketchup and mustard fingerprint on one of the bills.

Back at the pool June walked toward the snack bar smiling and talking to the patron. "She *is* getting so big..." The patron nodded. June, sweet as Southern iced tea, said, "Alright, see you soon now."

She turned to the snack bar window, fire in her eyes. "Time's up, Jafar."

"I thought I was Aladdin."

June shot Roheed an even angrier look. Roheed quivered.

She pulled out her cell phone. "It looks like I need to make an anonymous call to the health inspector."

Just then Charlie walked through the door with a huge box of twenty-four-ounce cups, totally out of breath. "Man, either I am out of shape or these twenty-four-ounce cups are los populares!"

"Twenty-*four*-ounce cups?" June slit her eyes in suspicion. "Roheed said twenty ounce."

Roheed knew the jig was up.

Charlie shrugged nonchalantly. "Like Abraham Lincoln once said, 'Go big or go home.' "

If June were a robot, her head would have exploded. Instead, since she was a human woman, she just opened her mouth to speak, shook her head and walked away.

• • •

Later that afternoon...

Jonathan wasn't wearing a watch, so all he could be sure of was that it was about a hair past the freckle when he walked into the guard office. Judas was still asleep on the cot with beer cans scattered about.

"Judas, rise and shine. Time to train."

Judas grumbled and sat up. He picked up a couple empty cans until he found one with some liquid in it. He took a swig and spit it back out.

"Oh, yeah, that's the one I peed in."

A few moments later, on the pool deck, Jonathan stood before Florence, Judas and Roheed. Roheed was the only one not in a swimsuit. He was still wearing his work clothes.

Jonathan addressed his squad. "Alright, team, if we are going to be able to even think about starting to pretend that we have a one in a million chance of beginning to consider that we might win...we need to train."

He began walking down the short line of three, looking them in the eyes and barking orders like a colonel.

"In order to save this pool, we are going to need to be here every morning to do laps before Ruby's Swim & Sweat. We'll need to swim laps on our breaks from work and dream about swimming laps in our sleep. Whenever we sit down, it should be on someone's lap, and when we take drinks, we shall lap the liquid up into our mouths with our tongues like a cat. Today we will begin the most grueling conditioning that most of you have ever experienced in your life. Now get in the water and let's see what you can do."

Judas raised a finger. "What about Rasheed?"

"Seriously?" Roheed said.

"What?"

"My name is Roheed."

Judas shrugged. "Whatever."

"He has to work in the snack bar for now. He's more advanced than the rest of us so he can afford to miss a couple practices."

"Really?" Florence was surprised.

Roheed blushed. "Yeah, well, I better go. Those fries aren't going to cheese themselves."

Jonathan dove in and powered through the water, hit the wall, and swam back to the edge of the pool. He wiped his face with his hand.

Florence stood poised to dive in. "I didn't expect you to be so fast."

Jonathan shook some water out of his ear. "I love to swim. I practically live at the pool...in the pool I mean."

And so practice began. Florence dove in and began swimming lap after lap. Judas crushed a brew, lowered himself into the water and started swimming expertly. Roheed watched from the picnic area near the snack bar. Charlie walked up behind him.

Roheed grumbled, "How is Judas so good at swimming? He just woke up from an alcohol coma."

"I think his frat has a water polo team. You getting in?"

"I have tennis elbow. I'll start training with them soon."

"Okay."

Roheed entered the snack bar.

Jonathan bounded up to Charlie, dripping wet from the pool. "You alright?"

"Yeah, yeah. Thanks for helping me out today."

"Anything I can do to help. So your dad thinks you work somewhere else?"

Charlie nodded.

"Here's my advice: Be true to yourself, do what you love, and work hard at it. And if that thing that you love just so happens to be working at the snack bar, so be it. Your dad will come around eventually."

"That's not exactly it, but thanks. I smell what you're cooking."

"That's what I'm here for, buddy." Jonathan spread his arms.

"You're soaking wet."

"Come on."

Jonathan pulled Charlie in for a big hug.

Charlie wanted to be annoyed but couldn't help but smile big-and-goofy style. "Get off me, you big creeper."

Jonathan just squeezed tighter.

CHAPTER 14

THE NEXT COUPLE of weeks flew by. If this whole thing were shot as a movie, those weeks would be the portion where the story progressed and was heightened through a series of different but related images, probably with an awesome song behind them like "Eye Of The Tiger" or Gwen Stefani's "Hollaback Girl"—you know, true classics.

So hum "Hollaback Girl" to yourself and visualize the following snapshots:

Jonathan showing his team a flyer announcing that the Tri-County Relay Race would take place in two weeks.

In the dead of night, Roheed walking through the guard gate and knocking on the guard office door. Jonathan appearing instantly.

Florence stretching out in her bathing suit, catching some rays. Judas lowering his sunglasses and checking her out from the guard chair. Her feeling his eyes on her and looking at him. Him raising and lowering his eyebrows in a confident manner. Her rolling her eyes and doing the international "barf" sign.

Roheed doggy paddling pathetically. Jonathan shaking his head and demonstrating the proper technique.

Judas, shirt off, sweating and muscular, doing push-ups in an obvious attempt to catch Florence's eye. Her taking no notice.

Roheed holding his nose with two fingers and blowing bubbles with his mouth underwater. Jonathan putting his head in the water and blowing bubbles without holding his nose. Roheed smiling and nodding. Roheed putting his head under the water without holding his nose.

Moments later Jonathan giving Roheed CPR until he sputters and spits up the water he'd swallowed.

Jonathan, Florence and Judas swimming lap after lap. Roheed watching.

At night Roheed feebly swimming once across the length of the pool and gasping for air at the other end.

Jonathan applauding.

And again, if this were a movie, but it's not, but if it were, *because* the movie would be set in Yellow County, Maryland, there would be an obligatory scene of our cast eating steamed blue crabs, covered in Old Bay seasoning, and everyone of age would be drinking Natty Bohs and maybe UTZ would do some product placement. Charlie and Judas would expertly insert their knives and gut the things, pulling the legs off and diving into the sweet, white meat, while Roheed would hammer the thing, not knowing what to do, until Florence would take pity on him and give him a picking lesson. Close-up shots would show greasy fingers dipping pinches of meat into hot butter and cold vinegar. And that scene would show that Florence was warming up to Roheed and that the team was growing together and we, as the audience, would think for just a second that this ragtag group of misfits might actually have a shot at preserving this utopia that Bill had tig welded together.

That's probably where the montage would end, and we'd jump right back into the story as the music ended and the last shot faded out on the glorious pool compound at dusk just as the sun was going down. Magic hour.

CHAPTER 15

IT WAS EVENING after a good, solid pool day. Yellow County had won their tennis meet against Glenarden, which took them down a peg because they had spent all day bragging about how they just tied for second place as the safest community in Maryland. Freaking smug Glenarden. Jonathan had held an impromptu belly flop contest—the flopper with the reddest belly got a free chocolate ice cream taco. And the appropriately named Stephanie Heiney had worn the bathing suit with the bottoms that had a knack for wedgifying themselves in her ample posterior. You could almost hear Sisqo doing a one-handed cartwheel on the beach in delight as she walked by. So, all in all, like Ice Cube once put it, so correctly and concisely, it "was a good day."

Jonathan, Florence and Judas were stretching to prepare for that eve's swim practice. Charlie sat by the pool eating mozzarella sticks. Roheed brought him a dip cup of marinara sauce.

"Thanks, dude."

"I think I'll be able to practice with the team tomorrow morning. My swimmer's ear is clearing up."

"I thought it was tennis elbow."

"Right, and swimmer's ear."

"Are these really your ailments, or have you been playing too much Operation?"

"What?"

Jonathan walked over and said, "I say we figure out the relay order tonight."

Unbeknownst to the Yellow County crew, the Brown Town Hall and Recreation Relay Race Team watched them from the bushes bordering the pool compound. From afar they heard Jonathan coaching his team. They chuckled vilely and rubbed their dry-skinned hands together for several minutes until their laughter died and their hands were tingly from all the friction. An hour later, they slunk away into the twilight.

Practice was over. Jonathan and the team toweled off.

"I think we were looking pretty good out there," Jonathan said.

"Not good enough," Judas scoffed. "I'd still put my money on Brown Town. They have that chick with the fin."

"I know that probability is against us," Roheed said, "but dammit, every once in a while it's time for the one to happen in the one in a million chance."

Florence nodded. "I actually kind of agree."

"Really?" Roheed smiled like a goof.

"Okay, dudes." Judas continued with his negative Nancy 'tude. "Whatever. I'm still gonna update my resume for when this place shuts down."

"And what would be on that resume?" Roheed asked.

Florence almost smiled, seeing the set-up.

Judas, oblivious, said, "Crushing beers, hazing frosh, chasing tail...and data entry."

Roheed nodded. Florence bit her lip to keep from smiling.

"Anyway, you're going to have a whole month of being unemployed before school starts." Then Judas turned to Jonathan and said, "And you'll have a whole month of being unemployed before, uh...whatever it is that you do when you're not here...starts. Or finishes or whatever."

Jonathan waved an invisible white flag. "That's enough. We're meeting here early tomorrow morning, and we're training. That's it."

Minutes later, Judas and Florence each got in their cars. Judas sped off.

Florence pulled out of her space and drove down the road, slowly passing Roheed, who was walking on the sidewalk. He looked up hopefully. She avoided eye contact and kept driving.

Roheed sighed and continued to trudge home.

• • •

That night, Charlie again faced off against his typewriter. The page before him still read *FADE IN:* toward the top left corner. He typed fast and furiously for a single moment. He stopped and admired his handiwork.

The page then read *FADE IN:* and a couple lines under it, *INT.*

Charlie sighed, got up from his typewriter, and lay in bed.

• • •

Jonathan snored loudly on his cot in the guard office as Shannon, Channan, Carmichael, and Susan snuck into the YCCSRC compound. All dressed in black, they quickly and stealthily made their way to the edge of the pool, communicating using hand signals. The twins grabbed a thick hose and began emptying the pool.

When the pool was drained, Carmichael ran a hose up the stairs, out of the pool compound into a nearby hydrant that had been wrenched open. A larger than average wrench lay beside the hydrant on the grass. He began filling the pool with fresh water. Susan dumped in numerous twenty-pound bags of salt.

The twins carried a large fish tank between the two of them. Even if Jonathan were awake, it would have been too dark for him to see what floated in that aquarium.

When the Brown Towners were done, they covered their tracks. On their way out of the compound Susan glanced into the guard office and saw Jonathan sleeping. She motioned to the rest, and they all peered in, stifling their laughter. Channan snapped a couple pictures with his phone; then they all made like a couple of eggs at IHOP and scrammed.

• • •

The next morning Jonathan awoke bright and early. He yawned and stretched and tried to remember the weird dream he had had the night before but couldn't. It didn't bother him though.

CHAPTER 16

AND I THINK everyone had had weird dreams the night before in kind of a group-collective-consciousness-type deal. Charlie had that recurring nightmare where he was pushing a giant typewriter up a hill, only to find a giant at the top who rolled the thing back down. Roheed swam in a vast, dark ocean, waves crashing on top of him while girls with shark fins on their backs circled. Judas was funneling a never-ending beer. Even Florence, although she had taken a Xany and turned on her white noise machine (not that it played a steady, unvarying, unobtrusive sound, but rather that it played things that white people like, like NPR and Dave Matthews and podcasts about productivity)—even she had a weird dream where she posted a selfie on her Insta and didn't get that many "hearts."

But they had all awoken, unrested, taken their morning dumps and headed to the pool for practice. They were going to do a relay run-through at full speed. It was kind of a big deal for them.

Judas knelt by the pool. "I just gotta check the pH and chlorine count. You guys can stretch or something if you want."

"I'm gonna jump in and warm up a little bit," Florence said.

"Cool." Jonathan produced a small water-testing kit.

Florence jumped in the pool and shivered. "The water's colder today than ever! It's colder than the lake by my dad's winter house."

"Hmm, that's strange. It was so hot yesterday you would think the water would be warmer."

"I'm going to try to swim it out."

Jonathan looked at his water-test strip. "According to the test the chlorine count is zero?" He put his finger in the water and tasted it. "Is that salt?"

Under the surface of the water dozens of huge jellyfish floated slowly and rhythmically. Florence swam toward them unknowingly.

"The water looks weird." Jonathan squinted into the pool. "What are those white things?"

"Scyphozoa!" Roheed yelled.

Jonathan shook his head. "What?"

"Florence, look out...jellyfish!"

Florence swam right into a huge jellyfish. The tendrils grazed the length of her back. She screamed in pain. "What the... It burns!"

Roheed sprang into action and dove into the water. He blazed through the pool to Florence and grabbed her with one of his thin arms. The other arm propelled them to the edge of the pool, where he jumped out and helped her out gently, a sting wound already reddening on her lower back.

"It hurts," Florence whimpered.

"I don't think we have anything that will immediately stop the toxins except human urine," Jonathan offered.

"What?"

Judas's eyes widened. "Are you saying someone is going to have to pee-pee on Florence?"

"I'm afraid so," Jonathan said.

Judas, solemnly, said, "I volunteer as tribute." He dropped his swim trousers.

Roheed had to turn away.

Florence covered her ears and shut her eyes.

As the deed was being done, Judas reflected, "You know, it's funny. This is the first time something has *stopped* burning when I pee."

...

Jonathan, Roheed, Judas and Charlie sat outside of the guard office at the guard table.

"Who do you think did it?" Charlie asked, even though he had a pretty good idea.

"Who knows?" Judas said. "Probably someone who hates Florence."

Jonathan put on his metaphorical thinking cap as well as a mesh trucker cap that said "Thinking" in bubble letters. "It was obviously someone, or a group of someones, who don't want us to train."

Roheed thought the answer was obvious and said, "Brown Town Hall and Recreation."

"I doubt it," said Judas defensively. "Why would they be worried about us?"

"Because we're getting good, dammit, damn good, and they damn well know it," said Jonathan damningly.

Judas continued, "But they have those twins that are into each other, the Olympics guy, *and* the chick with the shark back."

Jonathan stood up. "And we have an Eastern Indian kid with a set of big, shiny brass ones." He patted Roheed on the back. "He really saved Florence."

Charlie looked around. "Where is her majesty by the way?"

"In her fourth shower in a series of five showers to get Judas's urine off of her skin," Jonathan replied.

Florence walked out of the women's room and into the conversation, wearing a towel and shaking. "It was so warm...so warm." She shuddered.

"I'm glad you're semi-okay," Jonathan said to her; then he turned to everyone. "I don't want to be a jerk, but the race is tomorrow. We obviously can't open the pool as it is now. We have to drain the water, get the salt out of the drains, and restore the chlorination. If we don't fix this, we can't host the race and we're done. So let's get to work."

Judas pshaw-ed. "I've got a job interview at the Chain Male store. It's like Under Armour, only it showcases your abs better." And with that he walked away.

Jonathan and Charlie walked toward the pool, knowing

they had their work cut out for them, which seems like it should mean that their work was going to be easier because they already had their work cut out. Like, here's your work, oh good, it has already been cut out for you so all you have to do is complete it. The saying should be, you have your work, and it's not even cut out yet, so you have to cut it out and then complete it. But that might be a bit wordy...

Anywho, Florence approached Roheed, still wrapped in the towel. Roheed wasn't sure what, if anything, was underneath that towel clothing-wise, and that excited him, but he didn't have too much time to ponder it before she spoke.

"Thanks...for earlier," she said.

Roheed blushed. "I couldn't just see you in pain."

Florence began to smile but caught herself mid-smirk. "Don't think we're friends or anything just because you played hero for a minute."

She walked away, leaving Roheed feeling like he'd gotten his balls flicked.

CHAPTER 16 1/2

AS JUDAS INTERVIEWED at the Chain Male store in the Annapolis Mall, answering the question "What is your greatest weakness?" with a thinly veiled actual strength, "Sometimes I care too much about dry-fit exercise clothing," the rest of the team worked to get the pool back into swimmable shape.

Charlie scooped the jellyfish out with a huge net and deposited them into a trash can full of water, where they would be taken to a local sushi restaurant...to put into their aquarium, not to be eaten.

Roheed rigged hoses to drain the pool into the storm drain. Florence (out of the towel and back in clothes, to everyone's dismay) scraped salt out of a drain with a long brush, and Jonathan turned on the pool's water system to fill the pool.

As the water level rose slowly, Jonathan added chlorine and routinely checked the water with his testing kit. The team toiled, and the morning became the afternoon. Florence fell asleep on a deck chair.

At a certain point Jonathan shooed Charlie, Roheed and Florence away, promising that he would leave soon as well. But he continued to work.

The dusk predictably became the night.

Jonathan crawled into bed as the sun was just starting to peek above the horizon.

CHAPTER 17

THE SUN ROSE on the day of the Tri-County Relay Race. Jonathan slept hungrily as he had just gone to bed. He hadn't changed his clothes from the night before, so he was sweaty and dirty, salt comingling with the sleep that was crusting into the corners of his eyes.

His sleep didn't last long. When he awoke, he showered. When he came out of the men's room, he found June and a clipboard-toting Tri-County official standing with the box of his belongings.

Jonathan rubbed the water out of his left ear with his towel, and although no one had said anything yet, he broke the silence with, "Um, what?"

June was eager. "Well, hello, Mr. Poole," she said through a smile that only comes from sick satisfaction.

"I can explain—"

June cut him off. "No explanations necessary. Your cot, your things...I think what has been going on here is obvious."

"It was just last night. I had to get the pool ready for today, I swear."

But the writing was on the wall, like, not literally, it didn't say "Jonathan lives here" or anything like that, but once you had the idea that maybe a person was living in the guard office, you started to make connections like Bruce Willis at the end of *Unbreakable* when Sam Jackson was all like, "They call me Mr. Glass."

And June was a huge "b" word, yes, but no dummy, plus somehow she had received the picture that Channan had snapped of Jonathan sleeping in the guard office the night before last. "You're fired. Gather your things," she said.

Jonathan looked at the official. "He's already got my things, right? Or are there more things to pack up?" Then he realized the full extent of what was happening. He got angry.

"You can't do this. I've poured a lot of blood, sweat and tears into this pool." He looked at the official. "Not literally." Then he looked back at June. "I live and die by this club and the community that spends time here."

"Then maybe you should get a life," June sneered.

"I can't believe this. You're going to ruin everything I stood for, everything I've worked so hard for. The membership dues and profit margins aren't the problem. You're the problem. You're the reason membership is declining. No one wants to be around you!" His hands shook with anger.

June looked like she was going to be upset for half a jiff, but then just shrugged. "Be out by the end of the day."

"I can't believe this," Jonathan said.

The official had been staring at his shoes for most of the conversation, but at that moment he looked up hopefully. "The good news is your club has passed inspection. The Tri-County Relay Race festivities will go off without a hitch! Hurrah!"

Jonathan just glared at him.

• • •

Charlie woke up at his typewriter again, his back aching like a son of a witch. He looked at the page before him. It read: *FADE IN:* in the top left. *INT.* was whited out and *TITLE HERE:* had replaced it.

Charlie guessed that progress was progress. He didn't want to rush anything.

Then he heard a call from downstairs.

"Charlie," Art yelled. "We have to talk!"

• • •

Charlie walked into the kitchen with his trench coat costume on. Art and Hilda sat at the kitchen table, Hilda visibly nervous, tearing a paper napkin into long, thin strips, muttering something about Langoliers.

Art broke the silence. "You know, son, your mother and I were gracious enough to let you stay at our house this summer for free while you took an internship that would look good on your college applications."

Charlie went into BS mode. "And I can't thank you enough. I appreciate—"

Art stopped the BS mobile before Charlie could even get out of BS first gear. "However, that doesn't seem to be the case at all."

"What?"

"Come on, Charlie, the charade has gone on long enough. Open up that ridiculous coat."

"My coat?"

Art stood up from the table and approached Charlie. "And the worst thing is, I called that godforsaken Community Swim Club last night, and your mentor answered the phone. Or should I say manager?" He ripped open Charlie's coat and exposed that Charlie was wearing a bathing suit and his YCCSRC T-shirt, size M, for the SMedium amount of dignity he had left.

"It's casual Friday," Charlie offered.

"It's Saturday," Art said. "Starting Monday you're in the mailroom of my office every day until college starts."

"I don't know when that will be because I..." Charlie spoke quietly, "haven't finished my applications yet."

Hilda gasped.

"What?" Art said.

"I don't have a writing sample to get into film school."

"You won't even be attending school in the fall?"

"Maybe if they accept really late applications."

"Mailroom starting Monday. And you will be paying rent starting at the end of the month." Art was heated.

So was Charlie. "I'm not working at your office, or any other office for that matter, and I'm sure as hell not paying rent to live in my parents' house. I'm going to the pool."

"Don't expect to live here while you're still working at that dead-end."

"It might not be there after today anyway. I'm out of here."

"Give back your mother's car keys, too."

"Fine," Charlie yelled. He threw the keys onto the table and stormed out of the kitchen. In his room Charlie threw some stuff in a backpack and hoisted his huge typewriter under his arm. He slammed the front door behind him when he left.

Charlie trudged down the block with his load. Florence pulled up beside him, her car crawling as he walked.

"Hey, what's with the typewriter?"

"I just got kicked out of my parents' house basically forever."

"Aren't you pretty old anyway?"

"I guess," Charlie said. "Not really. I'm only eighteen."

"Ew." Florence grimaced.

"Whatever. Let's just get to this relay race so you can lose it and I can be homeless and sleep outside the Lincoln Memorial and write lousy poetry on this typewriter and then eventually have to use the paper to wipe myself."

"Okay," Florence said, but stopped and let Charlie in the car anyway.

• • •

Florence pulled up to the club. Other cars were already starting to arrive for the relay race, with license plates from such exotic locales as Virginia and Delaware. Swim teams from around the Tri-Counties and beyond were showing up in minivans wearing matching warm-up suits, goggles dangling from their necks.

Roheed was already there, standing by Jonathan in the guard office as Florence and Charlie walked in. Jonathan was taping up his box of belongings.

"What are you doing?" Charlie asked.

Jonathan didn't make eye contact. "I've been fired. I have to be out of here by the end of the day."

"Aren't you the majority owner though?" Charlie asked.

"Why do you have a toothbrush here?"

"Well," Jonathan said sheepishly, "it seems that even a fifty-one percent owner isn't allowed to secretly live on the pool grounds. The club just isn't zoned for it."

"You've been living here?" Florence asked, wide-eyed.

Jonathan nodded sadly. "I'm afraid so."

"Ew." Florence grimaced—again.

"I always wondered how you got here so early," Charlie mused.

Jonathan hoisted the box. "So I guess I'll be going now, never to return again."

"Maybe I'll come too," Charlie said dreamily. "We could get an apartment together. Or at least share a tent behind the Lincoln Memorial. I've got a ream of toilet paper in my bag."

"Now wait just a minute, everybody," Roheed piped up. "Jonathan, you said you have to be out by the end of the day, correct?"

"So?" Jonathan said.

"Only employees can participate in the race, Roheed." For some reason, Florence knew this.

Roheed continued, "Jonathan is still an employee until the end of the work day. Why not go out in a blaze of glory? Sure, we all may or may not be homeless and jobless tomorrow, but let's have one little taste of freedom before our lives go to hell. I have to go to college in a few weeks where God knows I'll be a complete loser. Florence will have to go back to...well, I guess being a sweet, wealthy, beautiful heiress with a popular Internet-based web show—"

"Sweet?" Florence perked up.

But Roheed kept right on going, "... who might have to fold clothes at the Salvation Army for a few days. And Charlie will have to take the Metro into DC and make friends with an already-established hobo who can protect him from the nightly hobo wars on the steps of the Lincoln Memorial. And Jonathan, you'll finally have to find a real job and stop living in a fantasy world of night swimming and public showers. And Judas... where's Judas?"

No one knew, but you know that thing where someone asks a question and no one knows the answer, but no one wants to be the one that says "I don't know" out loud, so everyone just kind of looks around and no one says anything, so the question just hangs there like Mr. Cooper until everyone just sort of moves on? Well, that happened.

Jonathan crinkled up his forehead into his thinkin' face. "What exactly are you saying?"

"I'm saying we suit up and take back this place that we love."

Charlie put a fist up in the air. "Yeah!"

Jonathan looked over at Charlie, grinning wide. "Does that mean you're joining the team, Charlie?"

Charlie's fist was still raised. "No!" He dropped the fist. "I don't swim, but thank you. I'm gonna go turn on the fryers and make some money and get us out of debt."

"Dang," Jonathan said, then looked around. "Alright, where *is* Judas?"

CHAPTER 18

EVERY YEAR THE Tri-County Relay Race was a grand affair. In fact, the very name Tri-County was a misnomer, a holdover from the days when just the counties Yellow, Prince George's and Montgomery competed. Today, nearly nine counties were represented, but the Tri-County Council had deliberated and decided that naming the race the Nona-County Relay Race would be a mistake. And they thought that maybe they would rethink the title once the tenth county threw their swim cap into the pool, because Deca-County sounded pretty sweet. They were big nerds, by the way.

To accommodate the race, the Yellow County Community Swim and Racquet Club was, as Chris Brown might say, on and poppin'. Red, white and blue flags hung across the width of the pool, two rows, so that savvy backstrokers would know how many strokes they had left before their hands would hit the wall on that final stretch. Vendors were set up around the property. Vivian Smythe, of course, was present, with her goddamned dog manicure business, as per usual, wearing a sweatsuit with something written on the butt, hair pulled back, big sunglasses on. Someone was making funnel cakes because, duh, and

Kumari's mom's shaved ice booth was nestled next to the snack bar. Families threw down blankets and towels and chairs and set up shop for an afternoon of healthy competition.

The teams in the relay race, Brown Town included, were starting to stretch near the pool. Fans congregated in sections to cheer on their club's teams. An announcer's desk had been set up near the guard office—basically a card table hooked up to a PA system. Two announcers, Chip Caldwell and Chad Chatterson, sat behind their microphones.

Chip and Chad were local podcasters, their most popular pod was a recap show where they discussed the latest installment of *Rich B Words*. They had a small but loyal following, and since they always offered to emcee the event for free and brought their own mics, there they were.

"Great turnout today here at the Yellow County Community Swim and Racquet Club, eh, Chad?"

"You got that right, Chip. All the teams seem to be in rare form, but I think all eyes are going to be focusing on the Brown and Yellow in the water today."

"Yes sir, Chad, the Yellow County Community Swim and Racquet Club and the Brown Town Hall and Recreation teams look as if they are in top physical condition."

The Brown Town team stood in its matching brown swimsuits, muscles glistening in the sun. Jonathan stood eating a hot dog. Roheed self-consciously crossed his arms over his skinny chest.

Jonathan looked over at Roheed. "Seriously, where is Judas?"

Roheed pointed across the way. "Is that him?"

It was indeed! Judas walked over to the Brown Town team and shook hands with Carmichael Schmelps. Judas and the Browns approached Jonathan, Florence and Roheed.

"What are you doing?" Jonathan asked Judas.

Judas cackled. "I work for Brown Town Hall and Recreation. I've been a spy for them all along...and also a third-shift lifeguard."

"Judas, you betrayed us?"

"They can actually give me a paycheck, which I need for my fraternity dues. They also gave me thirty Bacardi Silvers." Judas kissed Jonathan on the cheek and whispered in his ear,

"Forgive me."

Jonathan pushed Judas away. "What are we going to do now?"

Channan was already at the announcers' table, alerting Chip and Chad of the situation.

"Well, Chad, it seems that the Yellow County Community Team is going to have to bow out of the competition, seeing as they don't have enough swimmers."

"Golly, I love it when you're right, Chip. A complete relay racing team is four swimmers. It must really burn, too, being at your own pool and not being able to compete."

"Burn it must, Chad, burn it must. And as my favorite recording artist once said, famously, 'You have got to let it burn.'"

All was lost in that moment for our heroes. It was over. Only right then did Jonathan realize he was actually done living at the pool. He had thought that by some stroke of luck his team would win the race, and that the prize money would keep the club on track, that June would forgive him. But uh, yeah, nah.

Roheed looked at Florence. She was pissed that she was going to have to finish her community service at a non-poolside location, but actually, when she thought about it, she was actually more mad that she wasn't going to get to compete with her, dare she say, friends. And Roheed, because he had low self-esteem, thought about what he should have done better to prevent this from happening.

But then Charlie grabbed Chip's mic off of the table. "Actually, Chip, the Yellow County Team has four swimmers. Sign me up, boys." He dropped the mic, to both Chip's and Chad's dismay.

Chad looked at Chip. "Chip, do we look like the registration table?"

Chip readjusted his mic. "No, we do not, Chad. If that young man would like to race, he is going to have to first adjust his attitude, then make his way to the registration table by the shuffleboard area...."

Chip and Chad continued as Charlie walked down the steps to the pool deck where the rest of his team was standing.

"You haven't been training," Florence said.

"And you don't swim," Roheed added.

"I've never seen you in the water in all the years I've worked here," Jonathan said.

Charlie looked at them solemnly. "I don't need to train. And you are correct, I don't usually swim...because of these." He took off his shoes and revealed his webbed toes.

Susan Hark screamed, "They're hideous!"

Charlie ignored her. "I was born with webbed toes. They're embarrassing but they're like natural flippers."

"You're self-conscious about your toes?" Florence asked.

"Yeah," Charlie said. "They're weird."

The Tri-County official, who was quiet earlier in the day, was now in his element, feeling a little frisky. "Okay, everybody," he said, then looked at Charlie. "Frogger."

Charlie nodded, of course.

The official continued, "Let's get ready to race. I want a good clean race...which is going to be hard with Yellow and Brown in the pool!" A wide smiled cracked his face.

Chad jumped onto his mic. "I already made that joke earlier."

CHAPTER 19

LOOK, I COULD bore you with the details of the rest of the races that day, but we both know that the only relay that really mattered was Yellow County and Brown Town in the final heat, the main event, the grudge match, the ultimate, uh, thing! Moms who had been gossiping about the latest so and sos doing such and such, and even the dads who had been checking up on their fantasy baseball teams during their own sons' events, perked up. There was true competition in the air, and all humans can sense that.

Chad, sweating from the heat, choked up on the mic in anticipation. "Alright, Chip, folks, time for the real deal."

There were several other teams from other towns and cities that looked way less competitive than Yellow and Brown, but they had less on the line. They didn't want it, nay, need it like YCCSRC and BTHR did. Jonathan and Carmichael were poised, ready to dive in.

Chip quipped, "Chad, it seems that Brown Town Hall is making a surprise roster change."

Channan stood next to Shannon and Judas. "Okay, Judas. Good luck."

"Thanks, bro," Judas said. They slapped an intricate high-five.

Channan gave Shannon a "more than friends" kiss on the lips and ended it with a smack on her rump. Then he bowed out of the competition.

"Thanks, bro," Shannon said.

Judas tried his best to ignore the whole thing. He wasn't going to be the one to begin to unpack that creepy suitcase.

And then the crowd began to cheer, because this was it. The official gave the "on your mark" signal. He brought his arm down and blew a short blast on his whistle. Jonathan and Carmichael dove into the water and swam furiously. Carmichael got to the end of the lane first and did an effortless underwater flip turn. He began to blaze back down the lane toward his team. Jonathan got to the wall soon after Carmichael, but a sloppy non-flip turn cost him valuable seconds. He regained control and powered back. Carmichael got to the end of his lane first and touched the wall.

Susan Hark dove in with precision and began to cut through the water with her surgically enhanced dorsal finned back. Jonathan tapped the wall and Florence dove in. She gracefully swam to the end and back but lost even more ground to Hark.

The other relay teams were way behind, an afterthought in the mind of the crowd.

Judas looked over at Charlie before their teammates touched the wall. "Good luck, you duck-footed freak."

Charlie squinted into the distance. "Is that an underaged girl with a Smirnoff Ice?"

Judas looked and saw that there was no underaged girl with a Smirnoff Ice. He cursed himself for looking. The distraction gave Charlie a chance to dive in before Judas, even though Hark touched the wall before Florence. Charlie kicked his webbed feet like flippers and completed his lap in no time. Judas was quick but Charlie bought Yellow County valuable seconds.

Charlie tapped the wall and Roheed jumped into the pool. His goggles flipped up and water poured in. He corrected them as best as he could and started swimming. He was unsure and clumsy, quickly losing Charlie's gained seconds. Soon Shannon caught up and passed Roheed. She got to the other end of the pool and flip-turned with ease. She began her final leg. The crowd began to roar. Roheed reached the wall at the other end of the pool and turned around. Shannon was nearly halfway back to her team.

"It looks like Brown Town may have clinched this one, Chip."

"Clinched like my butt cheeks right now, Chad. Clinched like my butt cheeks."

"Indeed."

Charlie watched in horror. In that moment he knew that Yellow County was destined to lose, and shoot, he was going to have to work in his dad's mailroom. And he wasn't going to get into a film program; he was going to be one of those guys in his forties trying to get you to read his screenplay and talking about the web series he was trying to fund through Kickstarter. He hadn't written anything in his life, really, and all his ideas were trite, and...wait.

Charlie clicked on a little light bulb that happened to be hanging above his head at that moment. He turned to Florence, who was equally forlorn. "I have an idea. Florence, scream."

"What?" Florence was confused.

"I'm not the one who should be telling you this, but Roheed loves you in an almost, but not quite, creepy way. Remember how fast he was when you got stung?"

Florence nodded.

"Scream."

"Okay, um..." Florence began, half-speed, "Roheed! Help?"

"Louder," Charlie coached, "like you mean it."

"Help. Help! Roheed, help me, save me! I slipped and hit my head on the wall!"

Roheed looked up. Water obscured his vision. All he saw was a blurry blob waving its arm-shapes, but he heard Florence's voice.

"I'll save you, Florence," he said to himself, but also out loud, but he was underwater, so it just sounded like bubble-garble. Roheed kicked hard and swam literally like he'd never swam before. He caught up to Shannon at the last second.

Their hands hit the wall at the same time.

"It's too close to call from up here, Chad."

"Someone needs to get us the results, Chip."

"I concur, Chad."

Roheed jumped out of the water and tore off his goggles. He was confused to see Florence on dry land, perfectly fine, smiling.

"You're okay?"

"I can't believe that worked," she said.

"Someone just handed me a clipboard with the results, Chad. It looks like Brown Town Hall and Recreation..."

Jonathan hung his head. Carmichael Schmelps pumped his fist in triumph.

"... and Yellow County Community have tied? That's lame. What do we do with that big check, Chad?"

"It's cool, Chip. I brought my medium-sized checkbook just in case."

"Nice, Chad. I always underestimate you."

Judas threw up in a trash can. "I shouldn't have drank all those Bacardi Silvers before I swam."

Susan Hark pressed Carmichael up against a pole. "This is all your fault, Schmelps." She walked away.

Carmichael called after her, "I thought we were chums!"

CHAPTER 20

THE AWARDS CEREMONY commenced. A random team stood on the third-place podium. The second-place one was empty. Brown Town and Yellow County squished together on the first-place podium, obviously built to fit just one team. They each held a medium-sized check for five thousand dollars. A margarita machine with a large bow on it was off to the side, for some reason plugged in. Neon-green frozen liquid churned in the clear skull of the thing.

Chip addressed the crowd. "Chad, in a strange turn of events today, this year's Tri-County Relay Race is a tie."

"That's right, Chip. Last year's champions, the Brown Town Hall and Recreation, and the usually honorably mentionable Yellow County Community Swim and Racquet Club, have tied."

"Usually Brown Town just kicks everyone's ass, pardon my French."

"French pardoned, Chip. They'll split the prize money evenly between the two teams."

"I wonder which team is going to take home that frozen margarita machine."

Chad covered his mic with his hand. "Quiet, fool. I'll go start the car. You wheel it out and put it in the trunk." He uncovered the mic. "And we're done. Thanks for coming out today. Please pick up one piece of trash and throw it away on your way out." He ran out of there.

Chip slunk toward the margarita machine. The Yellow County team stepped off of the podium and congregated in the picnic area.

"I'm glad we tied and all," Charlie said, "and we worked together as a team and whatever, but we don't have enough money to cover the debts and the board."

"Plus I gotta get off the premises pretty soon," Jonathan added.

June walked up in a huff. She was wearing all brown and a pennant bearing the initials BTH&R was sticking out of her back pocket.

Charlie smirked. "You've been supporting Brown Town the whole time?"

"Of course," June said. "My babies work there, and they were on the team you just raced. How do you think I know so much about their business model?"

"Carmichael is your son?"

"No." June gestured to Shannon and Channan, who were sharing an ice cream cone, taking turns licking the quickly melting treat as it dripped down the sides. They saw June and waved.

"That can't be ethical," Roheed said, and everyone was unsure if he was talking about June's potential conflict of interest or the erotic frozen treat consumption that was taking place.

"Irrelevant," June said. "Jonathan broke the law by living on the premises. Everyone out before I call the authorities."

"You know what?" Jonathan spoke up. "You're right."

"I am?" June was surprised but pleased.

"She is?" Charlie was usually on top of things. He was bothered that they were slipping through the cracks.

"Yeah, she is," Jonathan said. "We all need to get the h-e-double diving boards out of here. Charlie, go to school and begin your real life. Florence, a couple of weeks at a thrift store would do you good. You need to learn how real people live outside of your fairytale life. Roheed, grow a pair. You're smart and funny, and quality girls will dig that. And I, I lived in a lifeguard office? Seriously?"

Jonathan took the whistle from around his neck. He put it in June's hand and said to her, "Take the pool. Make it however you think you want it to be."

And he said to the team, "It'll never be the same now that Bill's gone. But they can't change our memories of it, right? They can't change our memories of him. Let's get out of here."

Jonathan snatched the whistle back. "Actually, I'm keeping this."

Judas stood next to the pool, fully dressed in a Brown Town warm-up suit, listening to an MP3 player. Jonathan walked over and pushed him into the water. He grabbed his box of belongings and headed out the front gate.

Florence tapped Roheed on the shoulder.

"Hey."

"Hey."

"Um, do you think I could give you a ride home?"

Roheed smiled. "I would like that."

"Cool."

"I really thought you were in danger back there. I was about to kick some booty."

Florence chuckled. "You're cute."

Roheed and Florence walked out the front gate.

Jill sashayed over to Charlie. "If you're quitting, what will happen to us?"

"There definitely isn't and never will be an *us*, but you're going to the college in the community, right?

Jill nodded.

"So I'll see you around, and we can be friends."

Jill smiled.

"And as for me, this summer has really inspired me. I think that I can finally write that screenplay I've been trying so hard at." He gazed wistfully around the pool grounds. "Yep, and I think I have a pretty good idea of what it's going to be about, too...a pretty good idea."

EPILOGUE

COEDS STROLLED THROUGH the adequately landscaped quad of Yellow County Community College. A sign on the door to the auditorium read *Screenplay Table Read Today!!1 "In Sheep's Clothing" A script by Charlie Heralds*. Through that door was a long table where actors sat with scripts in hand. Charlie sat at the head of that table. A few scattered audience members, including Jonathan, Roheed, Florence, and Charlie's parents, Hilda and Art, sat in the stands.

Charlie read the scene action from his script. "Leonora hangs up the phone. She pulls out her calendar and checks the date the event planner gave her."

An actress read the character's lines. "The eighth, why does that date sound so familiar?"

Charlie read, "She flips to the eighth and gapes in horror."

The actress continued, "The eighth! The eighth is the next full moon. I can't put on a career-launching fashion show...if I'm a werewolf! Think Leonora, think."

The actress took a beat, pretending to think, think, think, like an awesome, acting-ass version of Winnie the Pooh, then continued reading, "I know. If I add rips and tears to the designs and I get werewolf masks from the costume shop, I can host my own show undetected."

Dramatic pause. The actress looked up from her script and stared into the audience.

"I just have to make sure I keep my thirst for blood at bay..."

And the *In Sheep's Clothing* table read went well enough. Charlie didn't want to beat himself up too bad. He was taking baby steps, but this was not what he had envisioned for his life, but he guessed that he was (relatively) young, and this was the first thing he had written, and, admittedly, it did kind of suck and the structure wasn't perfect, but he had put words on the page and done the proverbial damn thing, and dammit, he was damned proud of his damn self.

Art, along with Hilda balancing a tray of brownies in her arms, approached Charlie after the reading.

Charlie shrugged. "It's not USC or NYU or Boris, but at least I'm going to school, right?"

"I'm so proud of you. My tiny little grown man-child is finally growing up. I made you brownies!"

"Thanks, Mom."

Art pulled up the corners of his lips with his face muscles, "Congratulations, Charles. You worked hard, and you actually have something to show for it."

"Right. Well, I'll be applying to transfer as soon as possible."

"If this doesn't lead to anything, there's always that job in the mailroom."

Hilda held Art's arm. "Art..."

Art looked at her. "Just saying."

Charlie smiled. He stepped away and walked over to Roheed, Florence and Jonathan.

"I'm glad you guys came. What'd you think?"

"It was a tour de force," Roheed said.

"Great dialogue!" Jonathan added.

"Very promising." Roheed nodded.

"I thought it was going to be about something else," Jonathan said, "like this past summer, the relay race, us...but no, yeah, it was awesome."

A student approached Charlie and said, "I have a question."

Charlie turned to him and said, "One second," then turned

back to the gang. "Thanks again for coming. I hope to see you again soon. Come into Popcorn Movies whenever. I can get you free rentals."

They waved and walked away. Charlie turned back to the student.

"Yes?"

"You were delving into some pretty complex themes. I was wondering how you were able to relate so well to a werewolf."

"You see, I too used to have a secret I kept, much like the protagonist of my screenplay. I have webbed toes..." And he was off, already waxing poetic about his project.

Jonathan, Roheed and Florence paused by the door.

"We better head out," Roheed said. "We have a date." He smiled at Florence.

"Yeah, the team has practice in a bit. Good to see you though," Jonathan said.

"Totally," Florence agreed.

Roheed and Florence exited, hand in hand.

Jonathan headed out of the reception hall and into a long corridor where Chris the Diving Broad was waiting for him. She put her arm around his shoulders, and they walked outside through the quad. They stopped for a moment under a large tree and kissed passionately. When they pulled away from each other, Jonathan spit out a mouthful of tobacco juice.

"Babe, I thought you were going to cut down."

Chris smiled through a set of black-flecked tobacco-rich-stained teeth. "Get to work, hon. I'll see you at home in a few hours."

"Okay."

Jonathan walked across the quad to the campus fitness center. He walked past the front desk and gave a nod to Jill Bateman, the receptionist. She had a yellow legal pad with some scribbled song lyrics. Jonathan entered the Yellow County Community College Indoor Pool and Fitness Facility. He pulled on his YCCCIPFF windbreaker, size L for the large amount of respect he received while wearing it and even without it on. A dozen or so young men in swimming suits greeted him.

"Alright, team," Jonathan said. "The warm-up laps aren't going to swim themselves. Let's get in the pool. I want two hundred free and two hundred breast. Let's go!"

The young men lined up in their lanes, dove into the water, and began their practice. Jonathan took his whistle out of his pocket and slipped it around his neck. He began pacing the edge of the pool, yelling encouragement to the young men as they swam back and forth in the clear blue of the pool's over-chlorinated water.

CPSIA information can be obtained
at www.ICGtesting.com
Printed in the USA
BVHW031030311021
620380BV00007B/676

9 781633 931480